£ 2

"See beyond the surface
Believe in what you see."

Thomas Carpenter

"And I must be insane
To go skating on your name
And by tracing it twice
I fell through the ice
Of Alice"

Tom Waits

To Helen
and to my inspirational mother

First published in the UK in 2016
by Gresham House Studios Ltd.
Gresham House, Cornwall, PL18 9AB
www.greshamhousestudios.co.uk

ISBN: 978-0-9955717-0-9

Cover photographs and design by Peter Ursem.

Petrus Ursem

The Fortune
of the Seventh Stone

1 A Minor Repair

'Don't worry, Steven. It will be fine. The doctors know what they are doing. I'll be here when you come out again.'

His mum pulls him against her for a quick hug. He tries not to resist her, but it feels strange in the green hospital gown he's wearing. They've also given him a pair of plastic slippers. The slippers make a funny sound on the linoleum floors as he follows the nurse into the operating theatre. His mum is not allowed in anymore. She looks helpless, staying behind with the attempt of an encouraging smile on her face. Then the door closes and he is on his own.

'Climb on to that couch, love,' says the nurse.

He does as he's told.

'So, it's Steven, is it? Steven Honest?'

He nods.

'I need to ask you a few questions to make sure we have the right patient. Your date of birth?'

'September first, t-t-t-twothousand and one.' She puts a tick on her clipboard, ignoring his stammer.

'And the first line of your address?'

'G-G-G-Greystone House.'

'Perfect,' she replies. 'That is all as it should be.' She marks another tick on the clipboard and puts it away. 'Now, when you saw Dr Price a few weeks ago, did he explain the procedures to you? Did he tell you what we are going to do today?'

He thinks back to the appointment he and his mum

had with Dr Price, when the decision was made to have the operation. Dr Price was a tall man with white hair. He had called them into his office from the waiting room. A folder with various sheets of paper was lying open on his desk.

'Well then,' Doctor Price had started, looking only at his mum. 'Steven is thirteen years old. That is correct?' His mum nodded.

'Thirteen is the perfect age,' he said. 'We have the test results back and I'm pleased to say that they are all extremely positive. All the tests show that Steven has a perfectly healthy and normal brain, functioning on all accounts exactly as it should, apart from this little defect.'

'What defect?' he thought, but he kept his mouth shut.

'I must stress again that a stutter such as Steven has is not unusual in young children. But if you are still stuttering going into teenage years, I'm afraid the stutter is likely to stay, unless we do something about it, of course. You'd like that, wouldn't you?'

Dr Price now looked in his direction, but didn't wait for an answer. Steven didn't care. He was quite happy for his mum to do the talking.

'We know from research,' the doctor continued, 'that there is absolutely no connection between stuttering and intelligence. The brain scans confirm this.'

That was good news then.

'We also know it's a cause of embarrassment. Stutters often lead to teasing or bullying. Fortunately we now have the medical skills to do something about it, so there is no good reason not to. I strongly recommend surgery. It is a simple operation, a matter of reconnecting a couple of wires so to speak.'

He was trying to picture it, his brain opened up with a few wires hanging out. Something like an old fashioned computer with red and blue wires in a muddle.

'As I said, because the test results are positive and Steven is the right age, the outcomes are ninety nine point nine percent guaranteed. My advice is to go ahead with a corrective operation.'

He remembers that on hearing the word 'corrective' he realised this appointment was more serious than he wished. Did he want to be 'corrected'?

'Are there any risks?' his mum asked. 'Any side effects that we should be aware of?'

'Of course, with all surgery there is always a certain element of the unexpected,' said the doctor, 'but the scans are conclusive. For this type of operation we access the speech centre in the brain, located directly to the left of the semantic lobes. These lobes control how we understand the meaning of words. The medical literature mentions a very tiny possibility of so called 'enhanced imagination'. It only occurs if the lobes are accidentally touched. A chance of one in one hundred thousand. Speaking as a senior surgeon I must say that I have never actually encountered it. And even if this were to happen, who would object to a touch of enhanced imagination?'

The doctor smirked about his joke. Steven didn't laugh. Neither did mum. But the words 'enhanced imagination' echoed backwards and forwards through his head.

'In Steven's case, taking into account his age and healthy

matter as documented by our scans, I say there is nothing to worry about.'

Mum looked at him. Then she looked again at the doctor and nodded.

'Excellent,' said Doctor Price. 'We'll get a date in the diary.' He stood up and gave them both a hand, as if to seal the deal. His hand was cold. In a strange way it felt comforting, a hand of precision. He directed them back out of his office.

'My secretary will write to you to confirm our discussion today and notify you of date and time of the operation,' he said. 'Honestly, it will be just a minor repair.'

Had he seen the doctor smirk again when he said this?

That was three weeks ago. Now he is here in this hospital room, in a green gown and plastic slippers. He nods to the nurse. He isn't completely sure what procedures she's referring to and what's going to happen next, but it seems easier to pretend he's ok with it all.

'Perfect,' the nurse says again. 'If you're ready, I will take you through to next door, where we'll send you to sleep. Just lie down. I will open the big doors and wheel you through.'

In the room next door another nurse gives him a black balloon and tells him to blow in it. The taste of it is awful. After that things start to blur rapidly. The last thing he remembers is what seems like a chase through an endless corridor. There's a thunderous roar in his head. He's lying on his side, looking at the blurred metal bars of the hospital bed and people rushing past him with the speed of light. He wants them to stop. He wants everything to stop. He wants to climb off and find his clothes and go home. Then everything goes black and silent.

What Dr Price had said about the bullying was true. The week before the appointment he was walking home from his chess club. He was well on his way to becoming this year's champion. At the club nobody laughed at him when he made his move and said 'ch-ch-ch-check'. His opponents had other things to worry about at such time. 'Checkmate' always came fluently. It was the adrenaline of winning that eliminated stuttering.

He was walking along Harewood Road when Tony and Andrew, two boys from his new school, stepped in his way.

'Look who's here!' Tony said. 'It's ste-ste-Steven.'

'What have you bu-bu-bu-been up to?' Andrew demanded to know.

He tried to ignore them, but they blocked his way and wouldn't let him through. 'None of your bu-bu-bu-bu-business,' he said. He wanted to stand firm, but of course his unavoidable stutter instantly made things worse.

'Don't be scu-scu-scared st-st-st-Steven,' said Tony, putting it on even more. 'We are ju-ju-just interested in what's going o-o-o-o-on.'

Andrew stood grinning. 'Ju-ju-just interested mu-mu-mu-mate,' he repeated.

He worked out his options. Tony and Andrew were bigger than he was. They weren't likely to just let him go. Trying to reason with them was more or less pointless. His next stutter would only trigger more ridicule. Going back and choosing a different route home was a possibility, but against his pride. So instead he tried to push them aside and go straight through the middle - probably the worst choice. Andrew and Tony pushed him back easily.

'No touching st-st-Steven,' said Tony. 'No-no-no-no ta-ta-ta-touching.'

'Mustn't be st-st-st-stupid mate,' said Andrew. 'We only want to be fr-fr-friends.' Saying this they pushed him back into the prickly shrubs on the side of the road. There they left him and walked off. 'Ju-ju-just wanna be fr-fr-friends,' was the last thing he heard Tony say, and both of them laughing loudly.

He wasn't going to cry. He had become used to being targeted ever since his stuttering had developed. Having a stutter didn't make him stupid. He was probably ten times cleverer than Tony and Andrew together. They were older than the rest of their year. Tony was fourteen and Andrew was fifteen already. They just couldn't stand it that he was better at school stuff. That was why they tried to get at him. Yes, he did have a bad stutter, but was that his problem? Or was it everyone else's problem, everyone who had to be just that bit more patient to listen to him? He got up, brushed the dirt from his trousers and continued on his way home.

He doesn't know how much later it is when he becomes aware of a pink glow through his eyelids, slowly seeking its way into his skull. His eyelids give way and separate, and the glow becomes brighter. He opens his eyes fully and tries to focus. Where is he? There are white walls around him, wires and tubes and unfamiliar shapes, things with dials and displays. Sunlight is streaming into the room.

He moves his eyes and notices his mum. He turns his head towards her. Ouch, that hurts. She looks up from her magazine.

'Hello darling, welcome back,' she says. 'How do you feel?'

He wants to speak, but his mouth is so dry that he can't. She hands him a glass of juice with a straw.

'Here, let me raise you up.' She pushes a button to raise the head end of the bed, enough for him to have the drink without spilling it. He has a sensation of pressure in his head. He brings his hand up to feel it and discovers that his head is covered in bandages.

'They have kept you asleep a while longer,' his mum says. 'Just to make sure everything is alright.'

He finally realises where he is.

'What day is it?' His mum looks at him and smiles.

'Wednesday, sweetheart. It is Wednesday today.'

As she speaks Doctor Price walks into the room.

'Good afternoon,' he says. 'How is the young patient feeling?'

He picks up a clipboard from the foot end of his bed and glances over the notes.

'Have you found your speech back yet?'

He looks at his mum.

'Steven has only just woken up. He asked what day it is.'

'Excellent,' says Doctor Price. 'We don't expect Steven to be the greatest orator immediately, after having spent some days and nights in dreamland. No doubt it will start sooner rather than later. There will be no stopping what this young lad has to say. From my point of view the surgery was a hundred percent successful. As I expected it was a tidy piece of work. Healthy brain lobes, easy to spot the loose connection and simple to make the correction. We'll keep him here for another couple of nights to make sure the glue has proper time to set.'

The surgeon looks at him. His eyes don't smile.

'I'm confident he'll be home before the weekend. Then he can talk for England.'

He drops the clipboard back into its holder and leaves the room.

On Friday afternoon Steven is allowed to go home. Back at Greystone House he inspects himself in the bathroom mirror. His head still feels different. He has a small bald patch above his left ear. His mum says there's a scar – he can't see it in the mirror – but the stitches are already out and soon enough his hair will grow over it again. Strange to think that a bit of his skull bone under that scar is glued back into place. It's even stranger that his stammer has gone. He speaks to himself in the mirror, stringing together the trickiest words he can think of: 'Librarian, indecision, apricots, opening gambit, six o'clock news bulletin.' It all comes out fluently. It's weird to hear his voice like this, word after word, as if he has become someone else. 'Welcome back to Greystone House after a minor repair in your upper quarters.' His face looks different. The muscles in his lips, cheeks and chin don't seize up anymore. Is that face in the mirror definitely his, speaking without hesitation, without the repetition of any starting letters and syllables?

Dr Price had ordered that he should wait another week

before going back to school. He doesn't have to stay in bed but he must give his head rest, on the outside as well as the inside. Not easy to do! How can you stop your head from working, from thinking, especially when you're at home when everybody else is at school? He decides to ignore the doctor's advice. Instead he spends his days studying chess games and reading books. Kasparov, his five years old cat doesn't mind.

On the morning of Steven's eighth birthday his father had come into his room and put a big cardboard box on his bed. 'You'd better open this small present soon,' he had said. 'Otherwise it might go off.' He'd had no idea what could be inside and couldn't believe his eyes when he saw the little kitten peep up at him from the bottom of the box.

'What will you call it?' his father asked, when he carefully took the kitten into his arms. He knew the answer immediately: Kasparov, just like his great chess hero.

Two weeks later his father was dead. On a Saturday at four o'clock in the afternoon there was a knock on the door. His mum wasn't expecting anybody. His father wasn't due home until the evening. When she opened the door there were two police officers, bringing the news of the accident near London. At first she didn't believe them. His father had too much to do to suddenly die. He was always working on things in his studio, sometimes late into the night. He was always going to meetings and exhibitions, travelling to other cities and countries on his motorbike and coming back with a hundred and one stories to tell. He was always full of ideas and inspiration. He was too alive to be dead. It just wasn't possible.

But it was. The police officers said his mum should come with them. For identification, they said. He had to stay with neighbours. When his mum came back four hours later life had changed forever.

His mum is nothing like his dad was. She's quieter. She likes reading books and works in a library. But she really adored his dad. She always says that he was a real artist. The house is full of his paintings. There is also the big old fireplace in the sitting room. His father had carved the name of the house in the stone lintel over the opening in the chimney. 'Greystone House' it reads in impressive letters. When he was born his father had also carved his name and year of birth in the big slab of slate in the hearth. So there, right before the fireplace, is his name: Steven Honest, born in the year 2001. When he had just learned to read and write he was so proud to see his name in the floor. What better evidence that you exist, that you really are someone? Now he feels embarrassed about the letters being there and he is glad that they are covered up with a hearthrug. His mum still likes to look at the carving occasionally, but she also complains that ever since his dad had done it, the floorboards in the sitting room are forever creaking.

His dad used to tease him about his stuttering, but in the best way possible. His dad just didn't deny or ignore it. Sometimes he called him 'child of the devil'. He said that in old times people believed that you could recognise a devil, because there is always something wrong with a devilish creature, like a wonky eye or horns growing out of his head. But dad said it in such a way that he was in no doubt there was nothing at all wrong with him. His stutter was just part of him. Anyway, when they played a game of chess together Steven always had his revenge. Even when he was just seven his chess playing was already way above his dad's league.

In the weeks and months after his dad had died Kasparov had helped him through. The kitten just wanted to play and explore the world, be cuddled and fall asleep in his lap.

Kasparov now has the most perfect week with him at home. He spends most of his time in his lap, purring away. When he studies a game, Kasparov watches intently as he moves the pieces on the chessboard and yawns unashamedly when occasionally he says a sentence out loud to check if his stammer hasn't suddenly come back. He is getting used to this new voice, this new identity. He exposes his recovering brain cells to a flood of new information from his books, ignoring the medical advice. His mum has taken the week off work to look after him and wants to know all the time how he is feeling and if he isn't getting too tired from all that reading and chess playing. But he's not.

'Do you think you are ready to go back to go school tomorrow?' she asks on Sunday night.

His school is in Callingfield. He has to pick up the bus at the top of Harewood Hill, opposite the village hall where the chess club meet. His mum wants to drop him off to school on his first day back but he prefers to go by himself. It's only twenty minutes to the bus stop. Andrew and Tony will no longer be a problem. After all, they can't tease him anymore for having a stutter.

When he walks into the schoolyard he notices Isabella in a group of her friends. Isabella lives in the same village and was in his class in primary school, but they've only become friends since they found out they were in the same class in Callingfield. Last week Isabella dropped by one time after school. She asked how he was and when he answered her mouth had literally dropped open.

'You're not stuttering,' she said.

He replied in one long sentence, that – to be honest – he'd had lots of time to prepare for.

'No, I'm not stuttering, and I never will anymore, because a white haired doctor with cold hands who wasn't very friendly had a look at my massive brain and said there was nothing wrong with it except one loose connection which he fixed and he did a good job, even though he wasn't very friendly as I said before, and the operation can only be called a phenomenal success, because now I can say as many words as I like without repeating myself which makes it a lot easier for me to come to the point.'

During this statement Isabella stared at his face and mouth as if he was an alien from another planet. Then she started giggling.

'Maybe you'd better start reciting poetry, brain boy,' she said.

Isabella has of course told other classmates about the miraculous operation that cured his stutter. Others come to say hello.

'Can you say something, man?' says Joey.

'What would you like me to say?' He is prepared, ready to start talking about one of the books he'd read, but his first few words are convincing enough. It's true: in his former life, before the operation, he wouldn't have been able to even say those seven words without tripping over at least one of them.

'Wow man, no stutter,' Joey says. 'Congratulations, man!'

Steven is ready to give further proof of his fluency, but the school bell calls them in.

Their first class is history. Miss Henderson waits until they've all taken their places.

'Good morning,' she says. 'I hope you've had a lovely weekend and have enjoyed the beautiful autumn colours. And I hope you all had lots of fresh air, so that you're ready for a new week of useful study under my kind but firm supervision. And of course today we need to say a special good morning to Steven. Welcome back, Steven.'

She looks at him.

'Rumours go round that the hospital surgeons have performed a little magic to your already magnificent upper part. Is that correct?'

'Yes, Miss Henderson.'

He likes her. He likes the way she talks, almost mocking, but never for real.

'You need to give us a bit more than 'Yes, Miss Henderson', Steven. We want to hear for ourselves that your vocal imperfection has been repaired. We need hard evidence.'

'Well, Miss Henderson,' he says. 'I can say that I am delighted to be back at school, after my successful operation, and very much looking forward to submitting myself again, without delay, to your excellent tuition.'

Most of his classmates are grinning, some look in astonishment, not sure if he is the same Steven as before. He can still hardly believe it himself, to hear his voice come out so easily and in front of all his class mates. Tony and Andrew are the only ones who don't bother looking up. They just look bored.

'Thank you, Steven,' says Miss Henderson. 'That's all the evidence we need. It seems they did indeed get rid of your stutter. I'm quite sure that's not all you can say now and I shall have to watch out for this new word-ability that you display. I must hasten to add that of course there is nothing wrong with having a stammer. It happens to the very best. If however, as in your case, it can be helped through a simple operation, then why not? So congratulations, Steven. At least it will save us all quite a bit of time.'

This last remark causes a lot of giggling. He doesn't mind. Nothing will hurt him anymore.

All day long he feels inspired, flying on the confidence that he can now participate in a way he couldn't have done before. Miss Henderson talks about King Arthur and his Knights of the Round Table and wants to discuss whether the Knights really existed. Hard to imagine they hadn't. There were so many stories about the Knights' adventures to keep the kingdom safe. And what about the remains of Camelot at Tintagel on the north coast? Miss Henderson makes the point that legends often have historic facts entwined within them, although that doesn't necessarily make them true.

'On the other hand,' she argues, 'if stories aren't actual histories, that doesn't make them lies. There often is some element of truth in a legend.'

In the geography class with Mr Bakefield they look at how the different continents of the world are carried on different plates underneath. Mr Bakefield explains how these plates move around slowly, separating in some places and crashing into each other elsewhere. This has created pressures deep below the surface of the earth and earthquakes and volcanoes in some countries, whilst leaving rich layers of oils and minerals underground in other countries.

All through the day he has his hand up whenever he can. Perhaps Isabella is right, perhaps he is a bit of a brain box. Today he feels it's his right to be heard, to make up for all the times before his operation when he struggled to give clear answers.

It is one of the best schooldays he remembers. He has always liked school. There is so much that he wants to know more about. Have countries and continents really floated all over the globe like ships on an infinite ocean? Was England once connected to France, without a sea in between? Did it have a tropical climate? The world doesn't stand still, so much is clear. He wants to understand all he can about it. Where did it all begin and where is it all going? Without his stutter he's even more certain that the world is waiting for him, waiting for him to become a world explorer, or a scientist perhaps, someone to make important discoveries. Whatever it is – he's ready for it.

As he walks home he thinks about what Miss Henderson said about stories not being lies, even if they haven't actually happened. Would that make them half-truths, whatever that means? Could something be true and not true at the same time?

'Hello Steven.'

Tony and Andrew step out on to the road in front of him, just like the time before his operation. They have been waiting for him.

'What do you want?'

'What do we want?' says Tony. 'Nothing special. Just a little word with mu-mu-miracle man. We would like to see-see-see the mmmm-miracle for ourselves.'

'You can't get me with that any longer. I don't stutter anymore.'

'Well in that case, perhaps we should call you ta-ta-ta-teachers p-p-p-pet,' Andrew says.

They step up to him, forcing him backwards. His mind is racing. They clearly have no friendly intentions. How to get out of this situation now? He has to act quickly. He takes another couple of steps backwards. Then he turns around and runs. Tony tries to grab his sleeve, but he's too late. In a few seconds Steven is on the corner of Harewood Road and Church Lane, at the gate into the churchyard. He pushes the gate open and runs into the cemetery. Tony and Andrew are on his heels, but he manages to get far enough ahead to the other side of the old church and out of their sight.

'He can't escape,' he hears Tony shout. 'The only way out is through the gate. He has to come back this way if he wants to get home.'

Tony is right. Although he has got away from them, he's more or less trapped in the churchyard. He'll never be able to climb over the high stone wall on the other side. The only way out is the gate through which he came in. He moves from behind the church to a big gravestone on his left, large enough to hide him from view. Just in time because Andrew now appears behind the church.

'He's not here anymore,' Andrew shouts back at Tony. 'He must be hiding behind one of the stones. Keep your eye on the gate. Don't let him get out.'

But he has a plan now. Knowing roughly where Andrew and Tony are, he moves quickly from headstone to headstone, making sure he keeps out of sight. He needs to get closer to the entrance gate, but approach it from a different direction so that they don't expect him. Andrew mustn't spot him. Hopefully Tony will get bored waiting and stray further out from the gate.

It seems to work. After five minutes, hopping from gravestone to gravestone, he hears Tony again.

'Can you see him now?'

'I've lost him,' Andrew shouts back. 'He must be here somewhere.'

What he hopes for starts to happen. Tony moves some steps in Andrew's direction, leaving a bigger distance between him and the gate. If only he would step even further, but Tony keeps his eye on the exit and stays within running distance.

'Come back this way,' he calls to Andrew. 'We'll just

wait here until he shows himself.'

He has no intention of waiting until the two of them are reunited. He decides to go for it and starts running towards the gate.

'There he is,' he hears Andrew shout from behind. 'Cut him off.'

He runs for his life. He is quicker than Tony and makes it back to the gate before him. But the gate doesn't open. Tony has tied up the rope around the gate. In the two seconds it takes him to realise why the gate doesn't move Tony is upon him, soon followed by Andrew. This time they hold him firmly.

'So teacher's pet decided to run,' says Andrew, half out of breath. He is pushed hard. Tony keeps hold of his arm.

'But teacher's pet got caught,' Andrew goes on, pushing him again, hard on his chest, forcing him further backwards. 'Teacher's pet is not so clever now, is he? Not clever enough now to escape his friends. No more miracles for teacher's pet now, what?'

'You're not my friends.'

'We're not your friends? But we would very much like to be friends, wouldn't we?'

Andrew pushes him again. He doesn't want to go down and he definitely doesn't want to hurt his head, but being forced backwards without seeing where he's going he loses his balance. He falls sideways to the left. He tries to free himself from Tony's grip to regain his balance, but Tony doesn't let go of his arm. He goes down in the worst possible way, his body half twisted. Before he can do anything his head hits a massive granite gravestone, right where he had his surgery. Instantly all goes black.

2 Dead Man's Word

The sound of church bells ringing pulls him back to his senses. A heavy drone of regular beats pierces through his unconscious mind. Come back Steven. Come back to the land of the living. When he finally opens his eyes the bells have fallen silent. He sees clouds, sky and treetops. His head hurts terribly. Where is he? He scrambles up and looks around him. The cemetery. Then all comes back to him. He checks for a sign of Tony and Andrew, but they're nowhere to be seen. The gate is slowly swinging on its hinges.

Steven gets on his feet. He feels dizzy and leans on the big granite stone that, some time earlier, his head was bashed against. The sickly feeling in his body recedes. Not the ache in his head though. He touches the left side of his head. There's a sticky lump in his hair and blood on his hands. Did he crack his skull bone? He makes his way to the churchyard gate, finding support on the gravestones and crosses. Gradually he dares trust his own legs again.

It takes him almost twice as long to drag himself back home. As soon as he passes the railway bridge he can see the house. It always looks big from a distance, showing up white against the greens of the surrounding fields and trees. As he gets closer Greystone House disappears from sight behind the slope of the hill. The last part of his walk home is an old path leading steeply up the hill, with trees and branches arching over it from both sides.

Every now and again Steven says something out loud,

checking if the blow to his head has not caused the return of his stutter. Fortunately that seems to be fine.

It's already dark when he's finally back home.

'Is that you Steven?' his mother calls out. 'Did you go home with Isabella? I was worried.'

'There you are,' she says when he steps into the kitchen. 'How was...' Then she sees the state he's in. 'Oh Steven, what has happened? What have you done?'

'They were waiting for me again. They were waiting in Harewood Road.'

'Who was waiting? What did they do to you?'

He tells her what happened in the cemetery, how Tony and Andrew pushed him, how he fell. 'I hope my head is going to be alright,' he says.

His mum sits him down in a chair in the middle of the kitchen and cleans his hair and head with a clean tea towel and luke warm water.

'It doesn't look too bad,' she says. 'It think it's only a graze. Do you have a headache? Do you feel anything strange?'

'It feels numb. Not as bad as before. I'm not stuttering. I think I'll be OK.'

'Good. You must keep calm for a while. Supper first, that will make you feel better. Then I'm going to phone the police.'

'No,' he says. 'There's no point.'

'Of course there is a point. If those boys think they can hurt you like that, they are mistaken. It could have been a lot worse. They could have killed you.'

'There is no point,' he says again. 'They will just deny it. It will be my word against theirs.'

But his mum is determined.

'Of course not,' she says. 'I shall call the police and you must tell them exactly what happened. They will want to know the truth.'

While he eats his mum picks up the phone. 'I want to report a crime,' she says. 'My son has been pushed to the ground and knocked unconscious by two boys from his class.'

He can't hear the response on the other side, but his mum gives more details.

'They pushed him and he fell, in the cemetery. As a result he hit his head on a gravestone.'

He listens as she answers more questions from the police officer on the line.

'No, he can't speak on the phone now,' she says. 'He needs to stay calm. He's just had an operation.' She finally puts the phone down and tells him that the officer is going to come by tomorrow morning to take a statement.

The ache in his head gradually clears. There's a stinging feeling around the graze, but other than that he seems to have escaped without major damage to his head, on the outside or the inside. He keeps thinking about what happened in the cemetery. He knows Tony and Andrew are just picking on him because he likes school and they don't. He's not frightened of them. At the same time he can't deny that they're much stronger and it is two against one. Are they going to try to get him again? They called him teacher's pet. Stupid idiots! What's wrong with getting on well with Miss Henderson or the other teachers?

The next morning at nine o'clock a police car comes up the drive. His mum has already phoned school to let them know that he had a fall the previous day and needs to see the doctor, that he's fine, but will come to school a little later. He insisted that she wouldn't tell what really happened. She also phoned her work – the library in Plymouth – to say she'll be late too.

'Bumpy ride,' says the police officer as he steps through the door, referring to the stone track to their house. His mum shows him into the sitting room. The floorboards creak as the police officer sits down. He'll probably make the usual comment about that as well. He doesn't. He just asks him to go over what happened at the cemetery. Every now and then the police officer interrupts him with a question and scribbles in his notebook.

'I can show you where it happened,' Steven says.

'I don't think that will be necessary,' says the police officer. 'I know where the church is and I can picture what might have happened.'

Then the police officer tells him that he has already spoken to Andrew last night. It turns out that he knows Andrew's father, who runs a garage where the police motorbikes are serviced. Andrew of course denied any involvement. He said that he was playing football after school with Tony, on the other side of the village.

'You have given me a good account of what you say happened,' says the police officer. 'The problem for us with these incidents is that it's difficult to decide which account is most accurate. I'm not saying you're not telling the truth, but what your classmate told me could also be true. Nobody else was there you say, so I have nothing to go by except your story and his.'

Typical! Just as he expected.

'So the best thing I can advise you,' the officer continues, 'is that you take it a little easy for a while. I understand that you've had surgery recently? We will keep the notes on file of course. Perhaps you could travel to school with a friend?'

He just nods. He isn't even going to waste more words on the police officer. As he told his mum yesterday, what is the point?

The police officer wants a word with his mum alone. Steven is happy enough to leave the room. He has to get his school books together.

When he comes back down the stairs a few minutes later he hears the police officer's voice. He can't make out what he says, but his mum's response is clear enough.

'Steven is not a liar! He came home late yesterday afternoon. He was dizzy and had lots of blood in his hair. How else would you explain that? I cleaned his wound myself.'

Being next to the sitting room door he hears the officer's reply.

'Well, he could just have fallen, I suppose. I'm not making any accusations. Just keep an eye on him. That's all I wanted to say. Anyway, as I said, we'll keep the incident form on file of course.'

He makes sure he is out of the way when he hears his mum and the officer get up.

His mum drops him off to school.

'Are you alright Steven?' Miss Henderson asks, when he joins his class half way through the morning.

'Yes, Miss Henderson, thank you.'

'That's good, I'm pleased,' she says. 'Take your place. You can join in straight away. We are continuing with the lesson that we started yesterday, to see if we can find out what makes a story true and what would make it merely a fable.'

As he goes to his seat he glances in the direction of Tony and Andrew. Tony keeps his head down as if he's studying his book, but Andrew stares right back at him. He looks away. He hasn't made up his mind about what to say or do. A direct confrontation probably won't do any good.

After school he goes back with Isabella. From the bus stop in the village they walk to her home.

'So what actually happened?' she asks. 'Did you really just fall somewhere?'

'Not really! I was pushed. Tony and Andrew were waiting for me at Harewood Road. I tried to get rid of them and ran into the churchyard, but they blocked the exit. They pushed me and I hit my head against a gravestone.'

'Why didn't you say anything? I'm sure Miss Henderson would do something.'

'No point! Actually, my mother reported it to the police yesterday. An officer came this morning. That's why I was late. I told him what happened, but he didn't believe me. He knew Andrew's dad and had already phoned him. Andrew said that he and Tony were playing football. It was their word against mine. The police officer thought it was easier to believe them. No witnesses, you see. If I had said anything in school, it would have been the same.'

'That is so stupid. Of course you wouldn't make it up. Everyone knows that Tony and Andrew are liars.'

She really is on his side.

'They called me teacher's pet,' he says. 'First they teased me for my stutter. They can't do that anymore, so they have found something else.'

'What are you going to do?'

'I don't know yet. My mum is picking me up later. I need to ring her first.'

Isabella's mum is pleased to see her turn up with Steven. She's Italian. She tries to sound more English than the English, but even so, you can tell that she's Italian.

'That is so marvellous, Steven,' she says. 'The doctors in the hospital have made a miracle and fixed your stutter.'

Later that afternoon he phones his mum on his mobile to pick him up from Isabella's house. For the rest of the week she insists on dropping him off to school in the morning. The problem with the police officer's suggestion is that most of his class live in the village. Nobody is as far out as he. There is always that bit of walking to get to the bus stop.

'I hope that this will soon blow over,' says his mum. 'Sooner or later those boys must get tired of bothering you.'

For the rest of that week he hardly goes out, at least not on his own. No more trouble from Andrew and Tony. In school they all behave quite normally, if you can call ignoring one another normal. It almost seems as if that Monday afternoon nothing really happened. If it wasn't for the graze on his head, he might start believing it himself.

Maybe that's why he decides to go back to the churchyard on Saturday morning. To refresh his memory. Would Tony or Andrew be out there? Not much chance. They wouldn't expect him to come through Harewood Road on a Saturday. It's unlikely they'll be waiting for him today. Nevertheless he has to be alert and make sure that he'll spot them from sufficient distance to make his way back before they see him.

But there isn't a sign of them this morning. Of course! Andrew probably had to help in his father's garage business. Tony alone would be less of a problem. He still looks around him twice before he goes through the gate and enters the cemetery. It doesn't take him long to spot the massive granite gravestone, not far from the gate, with which he had such an unpleasant collision. It hurts to remember it. He inspects the stone for evidence, traces of his blood perhaps. Nothing. It's quite a plain stone, rectangular at its base and a half round curve at the top. There's a green sheen of moss over it. The stone stands motionless, as if it has nothing to do with him, as if nothing had happened five days ago. He takes a step back to read the inscription. The letters are so old that it isn't easy to make out, but after a while he can read what it says.

Here lies
Thomas Carpenter
Mine Captain
1812 – 1892

Mark a Dead Man's Word
Fortune by the Seventh Stone
Tin and Copper for the Lord
Silver underneath my Bones

And his Beloved Wife Clara
1814 – 1892
May they Rest in Peace

Strange inscription to put on a gravestone! What is a Mine Captain? There are many old mines around the village. There is one at Wheal Argon, in the small woodland opposite Greystone House. Old stone buildings half collapsed and overgrown with trees. So this man must have been some kind of worker in the mine, a tin and copper mine probably. It still doesn't make sense. Why put something like this on your gravestone?

'Anyway Thomas and Clara,' he says out loud, 'I hope my head bash didn't disturb your peace. For my part I am pleased that your stone didn't completely crack my skull.'

Then he turns around and walks back to the cemetery gate. Fortunately there's still no sign of Andrew or Tony.

Life gradually returns to a more regular pattern. Steven's hospital operation already seems a long time ago and speaking fluently now comes naturally. In the mornings his mum gives him a lift to school. In the afternoons he goes home with Isabella, before he continues the short walk from there to Greystone House alone. Should Andrew and Tony plan to come after him again, they can at least never be sure when to expect him. Should they be waiting for him, it would probably soon bore them and make them give up. Perhaps the phone call from the police officer has made them think twice. In any case, they don't trouble him any more that week, not after school and not on Friday afternoon, when he walks to and from the session at the chess club.

There's one thing however that he can't get out of his mind. The unusual inscription on that gravestone. As far as he knows inscriptions on a gravestone should express a religious message, or a wish that the person buried might safely arrive in the next world, or something like that. The text on this stone is different, as if it is some kind of joke. The only religious thing in it is the mention of the Lord, but why should God be given tin and copper? His mum says that a Mine Captain was a kind of foreman, not a miner who would go down to dig for minerals, but the manager in charge, somebody higher up. She brought him a library book about the local mines. Most of them were tin and copper mines, so that part of the inscription makes sense, but what about 'Silver underneath my Bones'? What about 'Fortune by the Seventh Stone'?

When the next Saturday comes Steven is irresistibly drawn to go back to the cemetery and read the inscription on that gravestone again. He wants to see the carved letters once more. Perhaps they'll suddenly make sense. He's still careful to avoid a new encounter with Andrew and Tony, but like the previous week the road is clear. He goes through the churchyard gate and straight to the granite gravestone of Thomas Carpenter. The inscription is exactly as he remembered. 'Mark a Dead Man's Word.' Some of the lettering is less clear because the green mossy growth has covered the carving, but the text is all there, definite and strange.

With his fingers he pulls at the moss on the stone. A strip of it comes away in his hand, revealing part of a symbol of a cross that he didn't notice before, under the words 'May they Rest in Peace'. So it's a proper religious gravestone after all. He clears away more of the green stuff. As he tries to get his finger under a thicker part the moss gives way and with it some of the granite. A section of the engraved cross falls down. He doesn't want to cause damage and picks up the granite chip to push it back in place. Then he sees something glistening in the small dark hole that has appeared in the gravestone. Curious now, rather than pushing the loose part of the stone back in place, he sticks his finger in the small gap. Suddenly the whole cross symbol comes loose. When he lifts it out the opening underneath is bigger and clean, a small horizontal void. In it he sees a small shiny object, not much bigger than a wax crayon.

3 Clarke & Liddell

The gap is just big enough for his thumb and finger. He carefully takes the object from the space in the gravestone. It's a cylinder, rounded at the ends. The metal is dull but in some places it really shines. Is it silver? He turns the cylinder in his hands. It has a join in the middle. He pulls both ends. They come apart and reveal a small parcel wrapped in browned newspaper. He unfolds it carefully. Inside the paper is another shiny object, some kind of pin. It looks like a key, not like a door key, but slender and more modern. What is it for? He looks at the gravestone again to see if there is a clue. He scans the edge of the grave, but it's all stone, impenetrable.

A sudden breeze makes him shudder. The weather is changing. A grey cloud glides over the cemetery. He rolls the object back into the paper, fits the wrapped up parcel back into the cylinder, closes it and puts it in his pocket. Then he pushes the stone cross back into the void, both parts of it, and he turns to go home. He makes it back home just before the rain comes thundering down on Greystone House.

'Where have you been?' his mum wants to know.

'Just outside.' He doesn't tell her what he has found. Not yet. He first wants to have another look at the object that is burning in his pocket. See if he can work out what it really is.

'I'm glad you're back. I need to go shopping. Do you want to come?'

'I'll stay here,' he says. 'I want to study a chess game.'

'Fine,' she says. 'I should be back in forty five minutes.'

As soon as he hears the door close behind her he takes the cylinder out of his pocket to look at it again. Apart from where it has lost its shine, the thing is smooth and finely finished. Who knows how long it has been hidden in that gravestone? Has it always been there, ever since the Mine Captain died? However long, it has lasted well. Perhaps it really is silver? He unrolls the newspaper parcel again. The object within is only a little shorter and thinner. It has a ball shape on one side and ridges and grooves on the other. He's convinced it is a key. But what good is a key if you don't know where the lock is? He studies the wrapping for a clue or a date, but it doesn't tell him much. It just looks old, a random bit of newspaper. The only words he can make out are 'Offices of Messrs Clarke & Liddell'. The rest of the print is unreadable. The ink of the letters has worn off in the cracks and folds of the paper. He turns the key around and around between his fingers. What should he do with it? Take it to a museum, to someone who will have a better idea what it is? Isn't it strange that this object was hidden in the gravestone that had knocked him out? He went back to search for evidence of the attack, not to find a silver object.

When he hears his mum return he puts the cylinder back in his pocket and quickly gets out his chess set. The rain has wrapped Greystone House in a grey curtain. He tries to concentrate on a Kasparov game, the one that made him world champion in 1985. But the cylinder and its content are all he really thinks about. If the object is a key, why was it hidden in that gravestone? Perhaps it's the key to a forgotten treasure chest, waiting somewhere deep in the earth for someone to dig it up. Perhaps the words on the gravestone are not a joke at all. Perhaps they are a message. 'Fortune by the Seventh Stone, Silver underneath my Bones, Mark a Dead Man's Word, Tin and Copper for the Lord'. The words keep spinning around and around in his head, however much he tries to push them aside.

The next day he phones Isabella.

'Isabella, it's me. I need to see you.'

'What for?' she says. 'It's Sunday morning and still quite early, if you hadn't noticed. I've only just got up.'

'I'll explain it when I see you. Can I come over?' She hears that he's serious.

'Give me twenty minutes,' she says.

Half an hour later the two of them sit in the sunroom at Isabella's. There are late tomatoes on the plants on the windowsills and the smell of the basil leaves in the October sunshine might have fooled anybody that this was Italy.

'My greenhouse,' explains Isabella's mum. 'Italian cooking needs lots of tomatoes and basilico.'

'So what is this all about?' says Isabella, when her mum has disappeared into the kitchen. 'Are you finally going to read me a poem?'

'I have something to show you.' He takes the cylinder from his pocket and opens his hand for Isabella to see the shiny silver object.

'What is it?'

'Remember what happened to me two weeks ago on my

first day back at school, when Tony and Andrew pushed me against a stone in the cemetery and that the police didn't believe me? So I went back to the cemetery last weekend. I found the gravestone where I blacked out. It had a strange verse written on it. The words were about silver and some kind of fortune. It was the grave of an old miner. At first I thought it was just a person who tried to be funny by leaving a silly rhyme on his gravestone, but I kept thinking about it. Yesterday I went back again. I pulled some of the moss off and then I found this hidden inside. I think it's a key.'

He opens the cylinder, unwraps the silver key inside and gives it to Isabella.

'Wow.' She takes the object and turns it around in her hand as he has done many times himself.

'It looks like a key,' she says.

'The problem is that we don't know what of, or where to find the lock. I've been wondering whether I should go to the museum to find someone who can tell me what it really is. On the other hand, if this thing has something to do with a fortune, I'd rather not tell anybody. At least not yet.'

'No, you mustn't,' she says quickly.

They sit staring at the thing. He suddenly feels embarrassed to have come.

'Can we go to the cemetery?' she asks. 'I would like to see the gravestone.'

When they come up to Church Lane they see from the rows of cars parked on the roadside that a service is taking place in the church. Of course! It's Sunday morning.

Steven looks at his watch. A quarter to eleven. The service probably wouldn't finish before eleven. The churchyard will be quiet for a little while longer, just enough time to show Isabella the gravestone. They slip through the gate and he leads her to the headstone. Isabella reads the names and the inscription.

'Look! His wife died in the same year.'

He hadn't noticed this before. Both Thomas Carpenter and his wife Clara had lived until 1892. Does it matter? He wants to show Isabella where he found the cylinder and pulls out the stone sections of the cross to reveal the space behind.

'Such a perfect hiding place,' she says. 'That space must have been made especially for it. It must have been there all the time.'

He walks around the grave again to search the edges for any possible clues. There has to be something. He feels the back of the stone with his hand. It seems completely smooth, at least as smooth as granite can be. Nothing that wants to let go.

'I suppose we'd better get back,' he says.

At that moment the church bells start to ring, marking the end of the service. Steven puts the two sections of the cross back into place. They fit easily and perfectly. As he turns Isabella stops him.

'Steven, look!'

She points at the cross shape, now back in position.

'What?' He's not sure what she wants him to see.

'The cross! It's not like an ordinary straight cross. The ends are made to look like bones. It's as the inscription says. Silver underneath my bones.'

He feels a rush of blood go to his face. The inscription isn't just a rhyme. It is true.

As the churchgoers start to appear from the service they hurry back to the gate, hoping not to raise suspicion, and join the crowd of leavers as if they are churchgoers too. Some steps ahead of them he recognises Tony. The grown-ups next to him are probably his parents. As Tony walks through the churchyard gate he looks around and glances briefly in their direction. Does he notice them?

Not much later he's back in the lovely smelling sunroom at Isabella's house. They haven't said much on the way back from the cemetery. Now he's bursting to share his thoughts.

'I hadn't noticed the bones in the cross,' he says. 'Do you realise what it means?'

'Of course! It means two things. Firstly it means that probably the cylinder is really made of silver, and that means that the words in the inscription on the gravestone are not a joke, but that they are true.'

'And if the words about the silver are true, the rest could be true too. There may be a fortune by the seventh stone.'

'There must be a fortune by the seventh stone!' says Isabella. They look at each other in amazement. Can it really be true that there is a treasure somewhere, lying ready to be discovered? By them?

'Perhaps the seventh stone is another gravestone in the cemetery?' he says. 'If it is, how do we find out which one?'

'There is a village not far from here called Sevenstones. You know, where they have the car boot sale on Saturday mornings. Maybe that has something to do with this.'

'Is there a row of stones there that we should investigate?'

'I'm not sure. There are so many stones everywhere in Cornwall.'

They sit in silence for a while. What next? As exciting as the possibility of a treasure is, what good is it if you have no idea where to start looking?

'Can I see the key again?'

He takes the cylinder from his pocket and hands it to her.

'I had hoped there would be a note or an instruction with it, but there isn't. Only an old bit of newspaper wrapping from which most words have disappeared.'

Isabella opens the cylinder and takes the key from the newspaper. She studies the print as he has already done himself.

Suddenly she says: 'What does it say here? Offices of Messrs Clarke & Liddell. It must be a clue! If this Thomas Carpenter has left a message carved on his gravestone, why wouldn't he give us another hint with this key?'

Steven thinks about it. He had thought those words on the wrapping were not important when he first saw them, but she might be right.

'Can we look up if there is such an office?'

'Yes!' She jumps up and returns with her laptop. She opens up the internet browser and types 'Clarke & Liddell' in the search box. Thousands of webpage suggestions come up, most of them with the word Clarke in bold.

'Try Liddell. That's a less common name.' But even for Liddell there are lots of references. Isabella scrolls through the list pages. No obvious connection stands out, but then he spots something.

'Hang on. This one says Liddell, Thornbridge. This could be something.'

She clicks on the link, which opens up a page with another long list of small print. It looks like a wall of words and letters without a way in, but Isabella points at the screen half way down the list. 'Mr Liddell, formerly Clarke and Liddell, Fore Street, Thornbridge.'

'I know where that is,' she says. 'That's that small lane at the top of the High Street where the second hand bookshop is.'

'Is there an office building in that street?'

'I have never noticed it. I wouldn't know. Maybe there was, once.'

It doesn't look very promising. But they're running out of ideas.

'I think,' he says, 'that the only thing we can do is go and see for ourselves. According to this webpage at least there was a Clarke & Liddell in Fore Street once. If it isn't there anymore we can ask in the bookshop. Or we can go to the library or the tourist information. Perhaps we can find someone who knows more about this office. It's the only thing we have right now.'

They have to be patient. On Wednesday afternoon they take the bus to Thornbridge. He knows the road reasonably well from car journeys with his mum, first across the river, then lots of sharp bends. Sitting high up in the bus it feels like a different journey. Or maybe it's just that he's not so sure anymore why he's going.

From the bus station they walk straight into town, past the imposing Town Hall and the covered market into the High Street. Isabella knows where she's going. Fore Street at the top is one of the older streets. It has cobbles, not very suitable for cars, and looks deserted, a kind of dead end street. There are some small shops, most of them old fashioned. The second hand bookshop is the second on the left. It has a display of interesting looking books in a bay window. He starts scanning both sides of the street for a sign of the 'Offices of Clarke and Liddell'. Isabella does the same. No result. They walk the length of the street, as short as it is.

'Let's ask in the bookshop,' says Isabella.

The bookshop is much bigger than it looks from the outside. Rows of shelves full of books fill the walls from floor to ceiling, leaving only narrow pathways to navigate your way through. There seems to be an endless number of small rooms, all of them bursting with books. In the middle of this labyrinth they find the shop owner behind a counter. He looks up from the volume on the desk.

'How can I help you?'

'We haven't really come to buy books,' says Isabella. 'We are looking for an office address in this street. Clarke and Liddell.'

'You've come to the right place. This shop used to be the offices of Clarke and Liddell, before I took over the premises, but that is more than twenty years ago.'

There it is! His hope crushed straight away.

'However, Mr Liddell still has a room upstairs. Do you have an appointment to see him?'

They both shake their heads.

'Well, in that case I suggest you go upstairs and knock on his door to find out whether he has time to see you. The staircase is there at the back, just behind the poetry shelves.'

Steven looks at Isabella. Have they struck lucky?

At the top of the stairs there's a landing with several doors. The last one on the right has a nameplate on it. Mr Liddell, Solicitor. Steven knocks on the door. No reply. He carefully opens the door and looks in. He sees an enormous desk and a small man with glasses and a thin, grey beard. The man at the desk almost disappears in the piles of papers in front and hasn't noticed him.

'Mr Liddell?' Now the man looks up.

'Hello,' he says. 'And who are you?'

'Steven,' he says. 'My name is Steven Honest.'

They both step into the room, but not much further than the door.

'I see you have brought a friend?'

'This is Isabella.'

'And what can I do for you two? It is not every day that I receive young people such as you here in my office.' He talks slowly with a breathy voice.

'Is this the office of Clarke and Liddell?' Isabella asks.

'Yes and no! Our offices used to be downstairs. Mr Clarke is no longer with us. He died a long time ago. So now it's only me, I'm afraid. I don't take any new cases, but I assume that isn't what you have come for.'

'We've come to ask for help. I found this.'

Steven takes the silver cylinder from his pocket and steps closer to the desk to show the man the cylinder in his open hand.

'There is a key inside. It is wrapped in old newspaper with your name printed on it. I mean with the name Clarke and Liddell. That's why we have come here.'

He takes the cylinder apart, unwraps the silver key and puts everything on the solicitor's desk. The old man's hands reach for the silver key. He brings it up to his face.

'Extraordinary,' he says. Then he smiles.

Isabella looks at him. She also doesn't seem to know what to think or what to expect.

'Did you say your name was Honest?' the man says. 'I hope you will be true to your name.'

The man stares at Steven intensely. It is as if he is searching him, as if he's trying to read his mind. Then suddenly he says: 'You see those shelves there in the corner?' He nods in the direction of the far end of the room. 'That small wooden box on the top shelf, get that down for me, if you please. Climb on the chair if you can't reach it.'

Steven moves a chair in front of the shelves, which are filled with files and documents. He takes the box that the solicitor pointed at. It is slim and it doesn't weigh much at all. It's made from dark wood, smooth and rounded at the corners. It's a plain box that could easily be overlooked, but he knows instantly that it's one of the most important things he has ever touched. He hands the box to the solicitor.

'This wooden box,' says Mr Liddell, 'has been in the care of this business for more than a century. I apologise that it is not in a safe, as it should have been. Our safe was too heavy to be moved up the stairs. Nevertheless, we have looked after it. Five generations of Clarke and Liddell have run this business before me. A certain Mr Carpenter left this box with my great-great-grandfather. It was given with strict instructions that it should be kept in the care of Clarke and Liddell Solicitors until a claimant would present the key to open it and as it passed through the generations in our firm those instructions were relayed and adhered to.'

The solicitor pauses and looks at him for a long time. Then he holds up the silver object and says:

'I believe that this is the key to open it.'

He pushes the key into a small circular opening at the front of the wooden box and turns it. They hear a soft click. The lid pops open.

4 The Last Will of Thomas Carpenter

'As I expected,' says Mr Liddell.

The wooden box stands on the large desk between them. It doesn't look that important. Why was it kept locked for more than a century in this boring office, or even in a safe downstairs? It is open now, but there's no treasure inside, no fortune, nothing but a bundle of some sheets of thick paper. Mr Liddell takes them out of the box and puts them in front of him.

'As I expected,' he says again. 'Why else would this box have been given into the care of our firm of solicitors? Why else were we paid to look after it?' He looks up at Isabella and him.

'As I expected, young man, these papers are the Last Will of Mr Thomas Carpenter. And since you are the one who presented me with the key that fits the lock, I have reason to believe that you will be the rightful heir to what may be determined in these papers. Please allow me.'

Before they can say anything, the old man sinks his eyes into the papers on his desk and starts reading, without saying any more. He, Steven, is to be a 'rightful heir', just because he found a key?

He looks at Isabella. She is staring at the papers on the table. She looks scared. Is he scared? Surprised would be a better word. How has he ended up sitting in this office, looking at an old solicitor reading a testament of which he is supposed to be the heir? Will this testament tell him anything more about the fortune?

Isabella looks at him, then back at the papers and the old

man reading. Steven is burning to know what is written down, but from their side of the desk, looking upside down at the old fashioned handwriting, it's difficult to make out any words. He assumes also that there might be some kind of formal procedure that has to be followed when a testament is being read. All he can do is wait until the solicitor is ready to share his findings with them.

It seems to take forever for Mr Liddell to work his way through the document. There is a smaller sealed document on the desk that the solicitor hasn't even touched yet. Finally the man takes his eyes off the papers and looks up. He clears his throat.

'Forgive me for taking time,' he says. 'My eyes need longer now that I'm old and this handwriting shows more artistry than what we are used to in today's world.'

He clears his throat again. They wait for what he's going to say about what he has just read. The solicitor straightens himself into a more upright position. When he continues his voice sounds different.

'As a representative of Messrs Clarke and Liddell, Solicitors, in accordance with the law of the United Kingdom of Great-Britain, and on the written instructions of the late Mr Thomas Carpenter of Wheal Argon, Cornwall, it is my legal duty that I, Mr John Liddell, Solicitor, relate statement of the Last Will of said Mr Thomas Carpenter of Wheal Argon, Cornwall, to his rightful heir, Mr Steven Honest, thereby witnessed by Miss ...'

He stops and looks at Isabella. 'What was your name, young lady?'

'Isabella,' she says, 'Isabella Carter.'

Steven's mind is racing. Wheal Argon? Did the solicitor say Wheal Argon? That's where he lives, at Greystone House. Is this a coincidence?

'... thereby witnessed by Miss Isabella Carter. This statement is read in the office of Mr John Liddell, Solicitor, formerly of Messrs Clarke and Liddell, at Fore Street, Thornbridge, on October the tenth, of the year two thousand and fourteen. As our law requires, the statement of the Last Will of said Mr Thomas Carpenter shall be read out in full to the appointed benefactor of the Will, in front of his or her appointed witness, after which we are able to act upon his instructions, within the limitations of the law and our professional capacities.'

He looks up again to see if they understand what he is saying. Steven is still none the wiser about where all this is going. It sounds serious enough. He just nods to make Mr Liddell continue. The man clears his throat again and now takes the document in front of him.

This is the true and lawful testament of the undersigned, Thomas Carpenter, of Wheal Argon, Cornwall, as drawn up by Mr Geoffrey Liddell of Messrs Clarke and Liddell, Solicitors, at their offices in Fore Street, Thornbridge, on June 6th, of the year eighteen hundred and ninety two. In this, my Will, it is determined that in the event of my death, by absence of a natural heir to my estate, my remaining belongings shall be gifted to the community of Lower Callick, with exception only of one part of my estate, of which further notification herein. I hereby appoint Messrs Clarke and Liddell, Solicitors, as the Executors of my Last Will, after my death.

I have always believed in the power and magic of words and have always enjoyed rhyme and riddle. People have considered me eccentric because of it. Mining, however, is a dangerous profession, for more than one reason. Looking into the earth changes your soul. It is as if looking into yourself. One must be strong of will to pursue and fearless to face whatever one finds down there, whether it is stone or fortune. What is fortune, what is wealth? No silver or gold is worth the life of a man. I have seen many perish, men and boys, in the chase for the tin and copper so much desired in our changing world. But not the workers risking their lives reap the reward. It is the landowner, his Lordship the Duke of Thornbyshire, who dines on the innocent lives being lost in the pit.

The mines are full of mystery. You don't always find what you are looking for, but those with eyes must learn to see. Almost forty years ago there were rumours that there might be tin or copper at Wheal Argon. I was one of the miners to first explore the site. We dug several shafts, hoping to locate a rich vein, as we did indeed, later, through the north shaft. However, I had been working on my own in the east shaft. I was alone and not working deep yet, not more than twenty fathoms. After several hours digging through a hard layer of rock suddenly a large stone fell away. Behind it appeared a natural chamber, a pocket of space encapsulated in the earth. I went in, using my lamp to see what lay behind. That is where I found fortune.

The object that I found there was not large in size, but I was soon to discover its enormous value. A mysterious treasure of a nature that I cannot here reveal, as that is the right and responsibility that I bestow upon my rightful heir.'

Mr Liddell looks up at them again, as if to check that they're still listening.

In April of this year my beloved Clara departed and as this testament is drawn up, I know that my own time is nigh. Our union was not blessed with children of our own, but it was blessed with love, and I will not be sad to join Clara in another world. When leaving this world my earthly possessions - as before mentioned – are to be gifted to the good people of Lower Callick. Only one part of my possessions, the treasure before spoken of, has been put in a secure place and can only be claimed by someone after me. The rightful heir to this treasure will be the key finder, he who has been chosen by fate or fortune, to discover the key to the casket that holds this, my Last Will. If you are the key finder, then know this:

    See beyond the surface
    believe in what you see
    a treasure lies safe, waiting
    to be found by my rightful heir,
    to be found by the seventh stone.

As I expressed before, I have always loved the magic of words. It is words that guard my treasure and words that will lead you to it. Don't expect silver or gold. Expect something infinitely more valuable. You have found the first stone. Now find the others. See and believe!

Signed: Thomas Carpenter

Mr Liddell finishes reading and looks up from the paper, but he doesn't say a word. Neither does Steven. Isabella seems as confused as he is. What they've just heard doesn't make any sense. It makes no sense at all. He looks back at Mr Liddell, hoping that he'll explain the meaning of what he has just read.

'I must be frank with you,' the solicitor says. 'This is one of the most unusual testaments I have come across. It seems that Mr Carpenter was indeed somewhat eccentric. Did you find the key yourself, young man?'

He nods.

'Can you tell me how or where you found it?'

He explains in a few sentences how he discovered the silver key in the gravestone after Andrew and Tony had attacked him.

'Right,' the solicitor says. 'So that seems to be the first stone mentioned in the testament. If things are as you describe, there is no doubt that you are indeed the chosen heir of Mr Carpenter. Whether this is by fate or fortune, as Mr Carpenter states, I don't know. At least I can close the case now, after more than a century, and register that the rightful heir has made himself known and claimed his inheritance.'

This is getting stupid. He can't control himself any longer.

'But there is nothing!'

He almost shouts.

'There is just a lot of talk about a treasure, but nothing else. How can I be the heir to Mr Carpenter's treasure, if there is nothing here? It's all just a joke!'

'Well, there is this.' The solicitor picks up the smaller

sealed document, which he has so far left untouched, and puts it in front of him. The outside is marked with words written by hand in big swirly letters. It says: 'Only to be opened by the key finder on acceptance of my inheritance.'

'What will it say?' asks Isabella.

'We don't know until it has been opened, but my guess would be that it could contain more of Mr Carpenter's words, perhaps another suggestion of finding out more about this mysterious treasure. It seems that Mr Carpenter was eccentricity itself and determined to set obstacles in the way for whoever wishes to claim the prize. This document can only be opened if you accept the inheritance.'

The confusion in Steven's mind is building rapidly. He's still trying to work out the meaning of the testament and the fact that he has suddenly become the heir to Mr Carpenter's treasure. Don't expect a fortune of silver or gold, the testament said, but something of much more value. He feels frustrated. He wants to know what's in the sealed document. Why can't it just be opened before he accepts it? What is he letting himself in for? Isn't it likely that the second document will only contain more words, more promises, but nothing that's real? How can he sign up to something he can't see or know first? Why him?

'What if I don't want to accept it?'

'Under normal circumstances, if the legal heir to an unclaimed inheritance has been identified, and he or she does not accept the inheritance, notice will be given in the local newspaper, enabling potential second in line claimants to come forward within two weeks.

If no claimants come forward the estate will then fall to the State, as represented by the government, and benefits distributed to charitable organisations. In this case however, as there are no real goods or benefits to be claimed and, as clearly stated in the testament, there are no other likely claimants, I would be justified not to give public notice, but simply close the case register and destroy the papers.'

'Destroy the papers?' Isabella says. 'But why? How?'

'These are simply the legal procedures,' Mr Liddell says. 'When a Last Will or a testament has been acted upon, in the sense that it has been opened and that the heirs have been notified of its particulars as I have just done with Steven here, when the instructions in the testament have been completed, the case can be closed. If Steven accepts the inheritance, I will be able to hand him this additional document for opening. I think you both understand that with that comes the responsibility to honour Mr Carpenter's wishes. It's not for nothing that a testament is called 'Last Will'. The problem in this case is that we don't yet know enough. As I have said already, I can only make a guess as to what further information it will contain. We don't know its value, if any at all, but we must assume that Mr Carpenter has not made his Will without reason. If on the other hand Steven instructs me that he does not wish to accept the inheritance the case will also be closed. I will record the decision in the legal register and get rid of the papers. In earlier times that would probably mean throw them on the fire. These days it is somewhat more trivial, I'm afraid. I will just feed them into the paper shredder.'

Mr Liddell looks at Steven. He stares at him, waiting for

an answer. Isabella looks at him too. He looks at his shoes on the carpet in front of the big desk. A silence thick as mist spreads through the room. His mind isn't quiet at all. Inside him a loud voice calls out: treasure, inheritance, adventure, the seventh stone. But another voice tells him it must be a joke. 'This can't be true. You are just Steven, you're not up to it. You had a stutter, remember? You can't do this. It's a joke. Somebody is trying to get at you. It's just a load of words.'

And however excited he is about an inheritance, a fortune perhaps, something to discover, the other voice doesn't give up and keeps repeating: 'You're not meant for this, it's a mistake, you're not good enough. Don't fall for it, someone is playing a trick on you.'

Eventually he looks up at the solicitor. The wooden box stands open on the desk. The papers are still under Mr Liddell's old hands, apart from the sealed paper in front of him, 'only to be opened by the key finder'. How can he be the rightful heir? Heir to what? Yes, he has found the key, or the key has found him. Surely that was nothing more than an absurd coincidence? What real connection does he, Steven, have to this Mr Carpenter, other than a painful memory of his gravestone? He read the words on the stone. Now there are more vague words or suggestions in this testament. 'Words that guard my treasure, but don't expect silver or gold.' It doesn't make any sense!

'I can't,' he says. 'I can't see how all of this can be anything other than wordplay, a stupid old joke. I didn't even know that this Mr Carpenter ever existed. It was purely a coincidence that I found this key. Why should I be his heir? It's only rhymes and riddles. They will probably lead to nothing. I don't have the time.'

'But Steven...' Isabella starts.

'Are you certain of this, young man?' says Mr Liddell. 'You don't receive an inheritance every day. Are you certain you don't want to give it second thought?'

He isn't certain at all. In his mind the conflict rages fiercely, with the different arguments repeating themselves over and over. But again, 'It's a joke, you can't do this' comes out on top. He just nods in response to the question.

'Very well, I can see that you have made up your mind.'

The solicitor sounds annoyed. He collects the papers in an orderly pile, including the sealed document. He doesn't put them back in the wooden box. He closes the box and hands it to him.

'I have no further need of this and since you own the key you might as well take the case. I will record your decision in the legal register and with that the case will be closed. And now, if you will excuse me, I must get on with some of my other work.'

Suddenly the meeting is over. Mr Liddell is already engrossed in another paper matter on his desk as if he has forgotten that Isabella and he are still in his room. They silently make their way back to the door and close it behind them carefully as they leave the room.

When they step outside on to the cobbles of Fore Street it has started raining. The cobbles are wet and shiny. They walk back to the bus station without a word. The rain comes down wetter and faster by the minute. Fortunately the bus back to Lower Callick is waiting in the station. They get in. Almost immediately the driver switches on the engine. The doors close.

Steven looks at his watch. It feels as if they have been in Thornbridge for almost the whole afternoon. It has hardly been more than an hour. Isabella has been ignoring him since they left the bookshop. She finally speaks.

'Why did you not accept it?'

'I don't know,' he says. 'I guess I woke up to reality. It all seems so far fetched and ridiculous. Why would someone who died more than a hundred years ago leave something to me, just because I happened to fall against his gravestone. He didn't even know that I would exist.'

'But you do exist and you did find the key to that wooden box,' she says.

'Yes, I do exist, but he couldn't have known that back then. If he wanted to gamble away his inheritance, whatever it might be, to a complete stranger some time in the future, why couldn't he just give it to me? He could have put it in a bank safe, or something like that. Why these riddles and this testament that doesn't make any sense? I don't believe in it. Somebody is playing a trick. I don't have time to try to solve puzzles from the past that will probably lead to nothing. I don't want to be made to look like a fool.'

'But we've got so far already finding the solicitor.' He can tell she tries to speak in a reasonable way, but she can't hide her frustration. 'Why didn't you at least open the sealed document?'

'That would have been wrong,' he says. 'Surely you agree that the whole testament was rather confused. It can't be anything other than one big joke.'

Is he trying to convince her? Is he trying to convince

himself? Isabella doesn't respond. There's little more to be said. He's made up his mind and he's going to stick to his decision, even though he knows she can't see why. Is he worried about not being able to solve new mysteries, or about the time it would take him, outside of school? Is he afraid to find out more? What does it matter? He just doesn't want to look stupid. This whole Thomas Carpenter thing must be some kind of enormous set-up. It has to be.

They don't say any more until the bus reaches the stop in Lower Callick. They both have to go their own way from here.

'See you tomorrow then,' says Isabella.

'Isabella, wait,' he says. 'I'm sorry. I mean, I'm sorry that I didn't accept it. I'm sorry I didn't want to go on with it, but thanks for coming with me and finding the solicitor.'

'It's OK,' she says. 'You are probably right. We have enough to do for school. So, see you tomorrow.'

'See you tomorrow,' he says.

Over the next couple of weeks the arrangements for going to and from school stay the same, to avoid new opportunities for Tony and Andrew to cause him trouble on his way home. He and Isabella spend time together in the afternoons, at Isabella's house. As by an unwritten and unspoken agreement they don't talk about their visit to Mr Liddell or the testament of Thomas Carpenter. Instead they talk about school and the subjects that Miss Henderson has brought up in her lessons. Sometimes they prepare their homework together. For some reason however, he doesn't feel the same enthusiasm as he felt on his first day back at school after his operation, when he was welcomed back as a talking miracle. Isabella doesn't give the impression that she desperately wants to work on school stuff together, but she is too nice to stop the arrangement.

Back at home in Greystone House Steven spends more time than he likes thinking about the visit to Mr Liddell. The wooden box in his room reminds him of the testament every day. He now keeps his chess pieces in it. Was he stupid to pull out, abandon the whole business? Time and again he asks himself that question. Every time he's perfectly able to reason himself back to normality. Mr Carpenter was just an eccentric. The testament, the way it was written, didn't make enough sense. It couldn't have been anything other than one big joke. It's better to concentrate on school and on his chess, rather than wasting time on bowing to a dead man's words that are probably nothing more than a fantasy.

Yet, however much he convinces himself that he has made the right decision, it's never completely satisfactory. Something keeps niggling in his mind. He can't help it. Was the whole thing really a coincidence? That Thomas Carpenter had lived in Wheal Argon, probably not far from where he lives now? In any case, it doesn't matter anymore, because as Mr Liddell said, the case is now closed and the papers are destroyed. Mr Carpenter's Last Will ended in Mr Liddell's office, and his very last words - the sealed document that he didn't read - will forever remain a mystery.

On Saturday morning he has a crazy dream. He is on horseback, riding fast. Behind him a vast landscape is on fire. He digs his heels in. Faster, faster, they need to go faster. He hears a voice call out to him. 'The truth, tell the truth, you must tell the truth.' Is it Mr Liddell, the solicitor? Then he is on a motorway, galloping behind a motorbike. He catches up and runs alongside the bike. It's his father, he knows it is, but he can't see a face underneath the helmet. Just as the rider turns his head towards him the motorbike slips away. There's no noise, it just slides away from him. He can't stop the horse. Suddenly there's a big black hole in front of him. His horse jumps, the hoofs stop moving, they just float through the dark night, waiting to land, but the landing never comes.

He wakes up with a shudder. It takes him a while to realise he has been dreaming. He hardly ever dreams. He smiles. Must be a taste of my enhanced imagination he tells himself. He's not good with horses anyway.

Later in the day he studies the chess puzzle in the local newspaper. White to force checkmate in three moves. He copies the diagram on to his own chessboard and checks whether he has set the pieces correctly. His eye falls on a small item in the newspaper column next to the chess diagram. Notice is given of the execution of the testament of Mr Thomas Carpenter, of Wheal Argon. He can feel his heart starting to pound in his throat when he reads on. Mr Liddell, Solicitor, Fore Street, Thornbridge, hereby gives public notice of the testament of Mr Thomas Carpenter, of Wheal Argon. The testament was released on October 10th, 2014. However, inheritance therein mentioned was not accepted by the first in line claimant. Any second or third in line claimants should come forward by October 26th. If by this date no claim has been made the testament will be closed and the inheritance, which is of insignificant value, released to the State.

He reads it again. This means that Mr Liddell must have changed his mind and has not destroyed the papers immediately. Maybe there is still a chance to change his mind? What's the date today? Saturday October 27th. Is it too late? He looks at his watch. Half past two. Is there still time?

'I'm at Isabella's,' he calls out to his mum as he leaves Greystone House, but he has no intention of going to see her. He runs to the bus stop. He is lucky. There's a bus at ten past three that will bring him into Thornbridge just after half past three. He should be at the solicitor's office at a quarter to four - if the solicitor will at least be there on a Saturday. In any case, he just has to go.

The bus leaves on time. At a quarter to four exactly he storms into the bookshop.

'I have come to see Mr Liddell.' He almost shouts the words to the bookshop owner. 'Is he here?'

The bookshop owner looks up from his book on the counter with a slightly annoyed look, just like three weeks earlier. Can't he tell that it's urgent?

'Mr Liddell has been busy lately,' he says. 'It took a lot of effort from the old man to finish his affairs.'

'Is he there? Is he working today?' he asks again.

The shopkeeper stares back at him. 'I am afraid that Mr Liddell has closed his business. All of last week I had removal men going up and down the stairs with boxes full of papers. Mr Liddell was here himself yesterday to hand back his office key.'

'He can't have left just like that! I need to see him urgently!'

'I am afraid you are too late,' says the man. 'He left yesterday. I don't know where to. He didn't leave an address.'

He looks around in desperation. He stares at the stairs and wants to go up to see for himself, to find Mr Liddell in his office, but he knows there's no point. He's too late. Without a word he turns back to the door, raging with fury. Why did he change his mind too late?

'Just one minute,' the shop owner says behind him.

He turns around.

'Were you not here about three weeks ago to see Mr Liddell?'

He nods.

'Is your name...?' The man pauses as he pulls a brown envelope from under the counter and reads what's written on it. 'Is your name Steven Honest?'

He nods again.

'In that case I have something for you. Mr Liddell asked me, should a boy with your name turn up and ask for him, to give you this.'

The bookshop owner hands him the brown envelope. He reads the words scribbled on the envelope - to be opened by Steven Honest only.

5 Isabella

'There's a moon over the river ...'

She goes over the words in her mind as she walks down the slope towards the Old Copperhouse where they rehearse with the band. At this point you can actually see the river in the village below, but there's no moon of course on a Saturday afternoon. She has never been completely sure of the name of their band. Blue River Dreams. It sounds too sweet and sentimental, dreamlike, whilst many songs in their repertoire are not at all like that. On the other hand, the name can be explained in different ways - blue river or blue dreams? - and in any case, none of the others in the band have reservations. Joey thinks it's a cool name. He always says: 'You start playing, you get into the music and the rhythm takes you wherever you want to go like the waves of the river.' Typical drummer! Marcus likes the colour blue and the fact that their name has a connection to the river in their village. The other band members, Rebecca and Simon, simply say they like 'Blue River Dreams' because it sounds good.

She spends most Saturday mornings going through her songs. She wants to be sure she knows her lyrics. She wants to be professional. It wouldn't be the end of the world if she didn't have all her lines from memory in rehearsal, but she likes to be prepared as best as she can. 'You must understand the lyrics inside out, not just the words, also the story. When you know the lyrics your singing can be expressive and free.' That's what her singing teacher says. The Thursday afternoon lessons really are the best moment in her week. In practically every lesson she feels that her voice is getting stronger. Sometimes singing really is like flying - flying away over the waves of a river. Perhaps their band name isn't so bad after all. Perhaps one day she could be a professional. She loves singing with the band. In less than a month from now they'll have their first real gig - playing at the Winter Fair in the courtyard at Oakendale Castle. Her cousin Sandy, who works at Oakendale, has invited Blue River Dreams to perform at the event. All the more reason to make sure she knows her words!

Despite herself she can't help thinking about Steven again and his unexpected change of heart in what she calls the 'Thomas Carpenter Affair'. She still can't understand that he decided not to take the papers. He clearly sensed her disappointment and although his apology at the end of the bus journey has at least cleared the air between them, it still feels as if the abandoned Thomas Carpenter Affair has changed their friendship. Perhaps the change started earlier, with his operation. Since he got rid of his stutter and talked faster their friendship had somehow also moved to a faster lane. There was less of a soft edge to him, less insecurity. She doesn't mind him being more astute, but that's why it surprised her all the more that he rejected the inheritance. Why did his sense of adventure suddenly dry up? What was he afraid of?

Last weekend, without telling Steven, she had gone to the car boot sale in Sevenstones, just to have a look around, hoping she would discover something that could relate to the words on the gravestone. She hoped that she might find a clue, that she would spot something to restart the fortune hunt, even without the testament papers. But there was nothing unusual at Sevenstones. Apart from the business of selling and buying old jigsaw puzzles, tired looking radios and battered crockery the hamlet was as dead as stone. Except that there was no remarkable stone to speak of, no legendary seventh stone rising above the earth as a silent message to those who are looking to see. She hadn't bothered telling him about her private investigation.

Anyway, it's all water under the bridge now. The Thomas Carpenter Affair is closed. If she and Steven have taken separate roads since then, that's just how it is.

Half an hour into the rehearsal she sings her heart out on 'Midnight Express', an old cover from the eighties that Joey has found, which he thinks is a good one for their gig. She loves the lyrics:

There's a moon over the river
There is silver in the sky
And I'm getting on this fast train
I've no need to say goodbye
Cause the world the world is waiting
Waiting for me to fly.

'That one is definitely in,' says Marcus when they end the song. 'Fabulous singing.'

Joey stands up behind his drum set, takes off the felt hat that he has recently started wearing, and lightly bows to her.

'Well sung, Bells,' he says. 'I think you have nailed that

one.' Simon and Rebecca also nod to her.

'Thanks guys, I just love that song. It really makes me feel as if I could fly, although I'm not in a rush to get away today. We have more practice to do.'

They rehearse for two full hours, working through their set list. They stop and start when they misunderstand one another, when the chords or rhythms don't immediately match up. Always there are things to sort out, but as soon as they start playing again they somehow synchronise and the music takes control of itself. She loves it when that happens. She's on great form and the afternoon flies by.

When they finish she hangs around to help Joey pack up his drums into their transport bags.

'I so hope we are going to do well at Oakendale Castle,' she says. 'Our first ever gig. We've got to get it right.'

'Sure we will, Bells. The way you were singing today, you'll blow them away.'

'Let's hope there will be someone to blow away. Let's hope the weather will be OK. If it is going to be too cold or wet, nobody will show up.'

'Good point! We need to do something about it. We need to have an audience, come rain or shine. We don't want to be playing just for our mums and dads.'

'I guess we could do a poster campaign,' she says.

'Cool. I like the idea of our faces grinning on every lamppost in the village. Fame at last! Bring it on!'

'I know! I can ask Steven to design a poster for us. I think he's good with graphics, and he owes me one.'

'How come?' Joey asks.

'Oh there is this...'

She hesitates. She had meant to say that Steven owes

her one because of this business of the Thomas Carpenter Affair. After all she had jumped into the adventure with him without hesitation, until he had suddenly cut it short. But she isn't sure now if she's supposed to talk about it - it has been a secret kept between the two of them. On the other hand, Joey is a friend and this whole Thomas Carpenter Affair is now finished business.

'Steven found this strange key on the cemetery,' she says. 'It wasn't like a normal key. It was proper silver, but wrapped in an old bit of newspaper. We thought at first it was a key to some kind of treasure box and then we discovered this old solicitor in Thornbridge, above the bookshop, because it turned out to be the key to a testament of an old miner. No treasure however, just lots of words. It was all quite exciting, but Steven gave up on it.'

Joey whistles between his teeth. 'Wow, Bells,' he says. 'Was it real?'

'I don't know. I would have liked to find out more, but he was probably right, that it wasn't worth the trouble. He doesn't really owe me one, but I'll ask him to help with the poster anyway. I'm sure he would like to do it.'

'How did it go?'

Isabella throws her coat on the hook and steps into the warm kitchen.

'Fab! We are going to do a poster campaign to let people know about our gig at Oakendale Castle. We need to have an audience.'

'Good idea,' her mum says without looking up. 'You don't want to play to the tree tops only.'

Her mum scrapes finely cut tomatoes and garlic from her cutting board into a deep pan with sizzling oil. The kitchen fills with sweet seductive smells that immediately make her feel hungry. Singing always makes her hungry and her mum's cooking is simply the best.

'By the way, Steven phoned for you half an hour ago. He asks if you can phone him back. But phone him later, supper is ready in ten minuti.' Mum can never resist spicing her English with Italian words.

'I'll phone him after supper,' she says. 'I need to speak to him anyway about these posters.'

Around seven that evening the phone rings.

'It's for you,' his mum calls out. 'It's Isabella.'

'I'll pick it up upstairs,' he calls back from his room. He picks up the phone and waits until he hears his mum put the receiver down.

'It's me,' Isabella says. 'I want to ask you something.'

'Me too.'

'What?'

'No, you first,' he says.

'It's about our band, Blue River Dreams,' she says. 'You know that we've been asked to play at the Winter Fair at Oakendale Castle? We need to have posters to make sure everybody knows about it. I wanted to ask if you could help us with that? We need to have photographs taken and made into a really good poster. It'll be our first gig. And you're good with graphics.'

'Of course,' he says. 'Thanks for asking. I'd happily do that. I'd love to make a poster for the band.'

'Great! Thanks.'

They're both silent for a few seconds. He doesn't want to barge in with his news, but she makes it easy for him.

'So, what did you want to ask me?'

'It's more something I wanted to tell you,' he says, 'about Thomas Carpenter and the inheritance. I was stupid about it.'

'No, you weren't. Don't worry about it. It was all a bit crazy and anyway, that's all finished now.'

'No, it isn't.'

'What do you mean?'

'Do you remember that the solicitor said he would destroy the papers? Well, he didn't. He did put a notification in the newspaper. I saw it by accident. The deadline was yesterday, but this afternoon I went back to Thornbridge. Mr Liddell wasn't there. He had closed his business but he had left an envelope for me with the bookshop owner.'

'With the testament?'

'The testament and the sealed document.'

Steven can't stop his voice sounding triumphant. That's how he feels, having changed his mind just in time to collect the Last Will of Thomas Carpenter.

'Did you open it? What's in it?'

'It's a verse, like the one on his gravestone, just four lines. It doesn't mention the treasure, but it talks about a second stone. It must be another clue.'

'Are you sure?'

'Pretty sure,' he says.

She remains silent on the other side of the phone. He knows he must give her some time to let it sink in. He knows she must already be considering what he hasn't even asked her yet. He knows he must give her time to think, but he can't.

'Isabella, I was stupid to say no to the inheritance at first,' he says. 'It may be just words, but it's too exciting to let go. I just couldn't stop thinking about it. I can't. Will you help me find the second stone?'

6 The Road to Penny Cross

Isabella takes him back to the sunroom. He probably looks ridiculously serious when he opens his bag and takes out the envelope with the inheritance documents. He can't help himself.

'I was worried yesterday that Mr Liddell wouldn't be there on a Saturday,' he says, repeating what he had already told her over the phone. 'It was worse even, because the man in the bookshop said that he had closed his business and that he had left completely. And then he gave me this envelope. Mr Liddell had guessed that I would come back and fortunately he had changed his mind about destroying the papers. After we had seen him I mean. He wrote a letter to me. Read this.'

He hands her the letter from the solicitor, a sheet of A4 paper, not in handwriting, but neatly typed and printed on both sides. Isabella takes it and starts reading. He reads along with her, even though he has read the letter so many times already that he knows almost exactly what it says.

Dear Steven Honest

You will see as you read this note, that, contrary to what I said during our meeting, I have decided not to destroy the papers relating to the testament of Mr Thomas Carpenter. Whereas I must wholeheartedly agree with you that the words written by Mr Carpenter in his Last Will are most unusual and way out of the ordinary, eccentric - call it what you will - I was nevertheless personally disappointed with your decision not to accept the inheritance. I'm aware that in writing this I am failing the professional code of my practice. In fact, I have no business writing this, but instead should be observing a professional distance from you, my client. However, this case has been in the care of Clarke & Liddell Solicitors for more than a century. Ever since I joined our firm as a qualified solicitor 50 years ago, no, ever since as a young boy I visited my father in his office, I was aware of the unopened wooden box and the mysteries contained within, that nobody could make a proper guess at. The Thomas Carpenter testament was, as a matter of fact, the very last case for our firm. There's no reason why you should know that Clarke & Liddell already ceased taking cases ten years ago. Since then I have only kept on the office for reasons of sentiment and to be able to look again over old cases. What else should an old solicitor do with his remaining time?

I digress. I always hoped that one day a claimant would come forward in respect of the Thomas Carpenter testament and enable me to complete this last remaining case, this last obligation of our firm.

Can you imagine my excitement and delight when on October 10th you appeared with your friend Isabella Carter to present me the key to that last remaining case? Your appearance at least gave me the satisfaction of unlocking the mystery, of at last opening that testament that had remained unread and unseen for so long.

If you will allow me, I must again express that the content of the testament is eccentric, but I believe it is intriguing too, in equal measure. It would be easy to dismiss Mr Carpenter's last statement as a delirious expression of an ailing and grieving old man, as words that are now without further consequence. However, and I state this as an ageing man myself, I would like to draw your attention to Mr Carpenter's comment on 'the power and magic of words'. It may well be, as you suspect, perhaps rightly so, that Mr Carpenter's eccentric rhymes will not lead to any treasure and that this so called inheritance is little more than an entertaining but ultimately worthless game. On the other hand it cannot be denied that words most certainly have power and meaning. As a solicitor my life has been dedicated to exploring and defending the relationship between words, such as these in Mr Carpenter's Last Will, and reality. The ownership of property, for example, can only be expressed in words on paper as recognised by the law and it is no coincidence that legal words such as 'deed' or 'act' refer to human actions. I digress again. All I mean to say is that we should not dismiss words outright, however strange they sound. We must give words a chance to speak to us.

It is therefore my firm belief that there is a case for subscribing to Mr Carpenter's challenge, if not to learn of a vague treasure, then at least to learn from his words and allow him the magic of his words. I also believe that it may not be a coincidence that it fell to you to find the key to unlocking this mystery. You will find this a strange confession from a solicitor, a man of act and fact, but as I have grown old, I have come to see more clearly that we human beings are only small specks of dust in the starry universe and that our course through life is not always our own to choose.

In short, I have not destroyed the papers as I said I would. I was hopeful you might change your mind. I kept the papers and placed a notification in the local paper, hoping to draw your attention. As in real terms the inheritance is of no *actual value I felt justified in taking this course of action. There would be little difference in destroying the papers or not.*

Ever since your visit on October 10th I have hoped you would return to my office with your mind changed, but you have not come, and I must now close my business completely. This note to you is the last encouragement I can make for you not to dismiss Mr Carpenter's Last Will. I leave the testament papers with my landlord in the bookshop and I have asked him to destroy all if you have still not come forward by the end of this year.

Yours respectfully

J Liddell, Solicitor

'Gosh,' says Isabella.

'I was so glad not to be too late. Mr Liddell clearly felt that I should have accepted the inheritance. I don't know why I didn't want to, at first. Thinking about it, even when it is all just a game, what do we have to lose?'

'That's true,' Isabella says.

She seems to hesitate. She doesn't sound completely convinced.

'And this is our next clue.' He unfolds the sealed document and holds it out for her to read the four lines written in the same handwriting as the testament papers.

On the Road to Penny Cross
No One Goes Alone
Eleven Giants and Five Dwarfs
Will Find the Second Stone

'Wow,' she says. 'It is just as cryptic as the words on the gravestone, this time spiced with some fairy tale stuff on top.'

'Those giants and dwarfs must be some kind of code. It must mean something else. Any ideas? What are you thinking?'

She sighs.

'Listen Steven, are you sure you want to do this?'

'Definite!'

'Last time you weren't sure! It is going to take a lot of time. Last time you didn't believe it was worth it.'

'I know,' he says. 'I think I wasn't sure that I was up to it. It all just seemed too much of a coincidence. I wasn't sure if I was the right person to take it on.'

'And now?'

'If I'm honest I still don't know whether it's all just a fantasy, just a silly game from Mr Eccentric Carpenter, but it seems a shame not to give it a go. Mr Liddell clearly thinks it's worth it. You never know what we'll discover. But ....'

He hesitates.

'I can't do it on my own. I really need your help. It sounds great, a fortune by the seventh stone, but we have no idea what or where it is.'

She looks at him. He feels nervous and drops his eyes, back to the paper in his hand. It feels like forever before she speaks again.

'OK,' she says. 'Count me in.'

He jumps up with relief and not knowing what to do next he suddenly gives her a hug.

'Thank you,' he says. 'I'm sure we can crack it between

us.'

'Are you having a party?' Isabella's mum comes in with two cups of tea. 'Something to celebrate?' Fortunately she's not really expecting an answer. He's not sure they should tell anyone about all this.

When they're alone again, Isabella says: 'I have to make a confession. That weekend after our visit to Mr Liddell, I went to Sevenstones by myself. I hoped that, if I could find a clue there, something obvious or strange, perhaps it would change your mind, even without the testament papers.'

'Did you? I mean did you find anything?'

'Nothing. I guess it would have been too easy. I hoped there could have been something there, a big stone in a field or something like that, simply because of the name of the village. I would have told you, of course.'

He's happy. So she wanted to be involved! The Thomas Carpenter affair has been on her mind just as much as it was on his.

'I agree,' he says. 'The name of that village could be relevant. On the other hand, it may just be a coincidence. I get the feeling that there isn't going to be a shortcut to Mr Carpenter's fortune.'

'If it really exists!'

'If it exists.' He repeats her words. They both stare at the paper in his hand. With only four lines of cryptic rhyme to guide them the task ahead suddenly seems impossible.

'So what is next?'

'I think we have to start with Penny Cross,' Isabella says. 'Penny Cross sounds like a place name. It has to be somewhere we can find. We'll worry about the giants and the dwarfs later.'

The next logical thing to do is an internet search. Isabella fetches her laptop. Steven thinks back to the morning when he showed her the silver key. They speculated about the 'fortune', the word so teasingly left on the gravestone, not knowing what to make of it. Now they're committing themselves. The evidence that it's not just a fantasy is here in front of them, in handwritten documents more than a hundred years old. Somehow these documents are telling him what to do. If they can work it out there is a fortune waiting to be claimed. By him! By law he is the rightful heir to the fortune, whatever it might be.

'Here we are - Pennycross,' Isabella says. She has her laptop on her knees. 'Looks like there is a school in Plymouth called Pennycross.'

'What is this?' He points to another reference on the screen with the word Pennycross in bold. 'Can you click on this?' A new page opens. It's a webpage showing a historical document about a church. He reads: 'Donations made to the church of St. Pancras, in Weston Peverel or Pennycross, for roof repairs, 1870. Building works overseen by the purser, Mr Brown. Saint Pancras, patron saint of children, was killed when he was 14 years old.'

'Ouch,' says Isabella.

'Hang on! Here it says: Saint Pancras is often depicted with a stone in his hand. We may have to make a trip to Plymouth.'

'I'm not convinced,' says Isabella. 'Do we have to go to a church simply because it's named after an ancient saint who sometimes picked up a stone? What business would Mr Carpenter have had all the way in Plymouth?'

'But it's at Pennycross!' he says. 'Unless there's another place with that name.' They look through more webpages, but there are no other sources that can reasonably be linked to their search term.

'Let me phone Sandy,' Isabella says. 'She studied history and knows a lot.'

'Who is Sandy?'

'My cousin. She works at the National Trust.'

He waits and listens to Isabella speaking to her cousin on the phone.

'Brilliantly,' he hears Isabella answer. 'We had a rehearsal yesterday. We have almost sorted out our set list. And we are going to make a poster. Is that OK?'

She is talking about the performance of her band.

'Great,' Isabella says. 'My friend Steven is designing it. We'll probably have it ready in a couple of weeks time. Sandy, I wanted to ask you something. You see a lot of the historical papers from around here, don't you? I wondered if you have read anything anywhere about a place called Penny Cross?'

He can't hear what the other voice says, but Isabella continues.

'It's something for school. It's a poetry project I'm working on with Steven. We had to study these old poems from a local man and one of the poems talks about the road to Penny Cross. We just wondered if that was a real place, or just symbolic for something else.'

She is careful. Not giving too much away. He likes that.

'Oh well, never mind. We'll have to work out something else about what it means, in the poem I mean. Thanks anyway, Sandy. And thanks for the photocopying too. I'll give you a call when the poster is ready.'

She puts the phone down.

'It was worth a try,' she says. 'She doesn't know of any place with that name. I thought that if anybody might have come across it, it would be Sandy. I suppose we're back to square one.'

They try to think of other options, different people to ask, doing a search in the library or some local archives perhaps. If only he could have asked Mr Liddell. The solicitor might know something about such a place. But the bookshop owner said that the solicitor had gone without leaving an address. Finally they decide that the church of St Pancras in Pennycross is more or less the only lead they have. Isabella is still not convinced but she agrees that a trip to Plymouth to investigate 'the scene' can't do any harm.

The frustrating thing is that they will have to wait until the weekend. What a drag! Right at the start their investigation seems to be reduced to being mostly guesswork and having to be patient. Walking back home he struggles not to feel down. Is it really worth it? But he is committed now. He has to be.

During schooldays they are both careful not to talk about the Thomas Carpenter Affair or 'TCA', as they have started referring to it. He likes this of her. She is in on the case, but she's also happy to keep it between them. They have their hands full anyway with their schoolwork in the run up to the end of the year. Miss Henderson, as nice a teacher as she is, can also be a demanding taskmaster expecting you to work for her lessons, and she's not the only one.

Isabella has her singing lesson on Thursday afternoon. She has just stepped outside when she hears her mum call after her.

'Izzie, on your way back, can you pick up the ham and sausages I ordered?'

'OK mum.' She closes the door behind her.

Her lesson flies by. As always the singing takes her mind to a different place altogether. She is no longer just Izzie from Kelly Road. It's not about wanting to be famous. It's more that she feels so much more true or pure. When she sings it feels as if everything she expresses is full of meaning. The better she sings the more it matters what she sings. It's just such a magical feeling.

When she walks past the butcher's window she suddenly remembers the ham and sausages. The old fashioned bell attached to the door clangs as she steps in. Mr Short appears from the cleaving room in the back. It's hard to imagine a better name for the butcher. He's not much taller than she is. He has short stubby hair, an enormous round tummy and a red face. His apron must have been white once. Now it's covered with old and new blood stains.

'Miss Carter,' he says. He's been in the village so long that he knows all his customers by name. 'You've come to pick up the sausages for your mother?'

'And the ham. She said she ordered sausages and ham.'

'Ham and sausages, precisely! I had already put them aside. Would you like them in a bag?' She nods.

Mr Short taps the keys of the till on his counter and produces a receipt. 'That makes four pounds and twenty pennies,' he says.

'I didn't bring any money. My mother didn't tell me.'

'No concern! I'll write it in the book. She can pay me next time.'

'Thank you, Mr Short.'

The butcher takes his credits book from the shelf to write in the owed amount. Isabella turns to leave the shop, but then she has a thought.

'Mr Short, have you ever heard of a place called Penny Cross?'

'Funny you should ask. I was just thinking about it earlier. I have to go there for a delivery today, after I close up. Bridge Farm. That was always called Penny Cross in the old times. You know, where the Turners live.'

'The Turners?' She doesn't mean to ask it as a question. Bridge Farm is where Tony lives, Tony Turner.

'That's right, the Turners,' says Mr Short. 'Unofficially it used to be called Penny Cross, before the bridge was built. You could cross the river there for a penny, in a little boat.'

'A boat?' She realises how dumb she must sound, repeating the butcher's words like a robot. 'That must have been fun!'

'Not sure you'd call it that. It was just the way people went from one side of the river to the other, at least when you were in a hurry. Poorer people couldn't afford it. They had to walk to the bridge at Horleycombe to cross the water. Now it's all a lot easier of course. Anyway, why do you ask?'

'No reason! I just read about it somewhere and wondered where it was. Anyway, thanks for the sausages.'

'And the ham,' he says as she leaves his shop. As soon as she's outside again she calls Steven on her mobile to tell him what she's found out.

'It was the way he said the word pennies,' she says. 'That made me think of asking him. He has been there for so long, he knows everything.'

'Great! So Penny Cross is at Bridge Farm, right under our noses. When can we go there?'

'There is one small problem,' she says. 'Bridge Farm is where Tony lives.'

'Tony Turner?'

'The same.'

He thinks about it, but not long.

'That shouldn't stop us,' he says. 'We may not have to go all the way to the farm. The road belongs to everyone.'

'Only thing is,' says Isabella, 'that since the bridge was built, that road only goes to the farm. Now that there is no ferry anymore, you only take that road if you need to be at Bridge Farm. It may look rather suspicious if they see us there without a proper reason.'

'We'll have to make something up,' he says. 'Or we could wait until Tony goes out.'

'That's it!' Her voice rings in his ear. 'Sunday morning! Do you remember that we saw Tony that morning you showed me the gravestone, coming out of the church with his parents? I'll bet he has to go to church with his parents every week. That could be our chance to have a look around without being noticed.'

They decide Sunday will be the day. They agree to meet on Sunday morning around ten o'clock at the foot of the bridge. With luck they could have a good hour to investigate the road at Penny Cross. At least it's better than going all the way up to Plymouth to look at that church. They can save that option for later.

On Sunday morning the early sunlight draws clouds of mist over the surface of the river. It's early November. Hurrying along Lower Kelly Steven notices that the river is more silver than blue in this light. Often it looks much darker and dangerous. In the summer you see people in their boats and even swimming in the water. Now at the start of the cold season the river is something different all together. It's a barrier between two sides. He shivers with the idea of being in the cold water.

Isabella is waiting for him under the arch. It's a good spot to look around without drawing attention. From here you can even see Bridge Farm on the other side.

'Sorry I'm late,' he says when he joins her under the arch. 'Kasparov had brought in a bird. I had to clean up the mess.'

Isabella points to the farm on the other side. 'I just saw them leave in their car,' she says. 'I think we guessed right. If they are on their way to church, they should be above our heads any minute now.'

Right on cue they hear the diesel roar of the car passing over the bridge some five metres above them. He steps out to see the Landrover of the Turners disappear in the distance.

'Coast is clear,' he says. 'Let's take our chance.'

The two of them climb the steps that go up to the road on the bridge above. There aren't many people or cars about at this time. They cross the bridge to the other side of the river and follow the road onwards as it heads into Devon and in the direction of Plymouth.

After a few hundred metres they reach the place where the track from Bridge Farm joins the new road. So this must have been the old road to Penny Cross. Since the bridge was built this old track has started to look like a private road, but Steven knows it isn't. They have every right to be here.

They can see the roof of the farm buildings towards the end of the track, closer to the river. Nearer by, about half way between the farm and where they are now, a chimney stack from one of the old mines rises up from the muddy fields, reaching much higher than a clump of trees nearby. The whole scene looks rather desolate and abandoned. Steven feels reassured that they've seen the Turners leave in their car. But nothing much around them gives him any obvious suggestion of what to do next.

'The difficulty is,' he says, 'that we don't really know what to look for.'

The track leading in the direction of Bridge Farm - Penny Cross - has grass borders with thorny hedges cut short for the winter and sections of stone walls. The stones are just piled up between the road and the fields. Going further down the track and towards the river the walls on both sides of the track become more dominant. They curve towards the farm. The track itself is getting muddier as they move closer. On the right hand side there's an old shed with a tin roof, looking as gloomy as the rest of this scene.

Isabella is looking left towards the river. 'Penny Cross must have been somewhere along here,' she says. 'It must have been a place where you could easily land a little boat.'

'I can't see anything unusual. It is just an ordinary track.'

'I guess it could have been further up. They must have a landing platform and a boat at the farm, being so close to the water.'

He repeats the lines of the second riddle to himself. 'On the Road to Penny Cross, No One Goes Alone. Eleven Giants and Five Dwarfs....' He stares at the walls on either side of the track.

'I've got it!' he shouts. 'It must be the stones in the walls. No one goes alone. Look how many stones there are. It must be the stones in the wall.'

Isabella immediately understands what he means.

'You're right,' she says. 'It must be the stones. These stone walls look pretty ancient. They must have been here in Thomas Carpenter's time.'

'So all we have to do now is find eleven giants and five dwarfs. Eleven big stones and five small ones! There must be a pattern.'

They start scanning the walls on both sides of the track for exceptionally big stones. It's easier said than done. The walls are cleverly built. When you look closer every stone seems to have its own precise place in the structure. Spotting a pattern in the stonework is a different thing. They go back to the beginning of the track to start their inspection anew and slowly walk again towards the riverbank and the farm. Isabella walks on the left. His eyes glide over the stony road banks hoping to detect irregularities. It makes him feel dizzy. There are quite a few giant stones and endless smaller ones, but none of them really shouts out to him. Without knowing precisely what to look for it's a random exercise. He's starting to feel desperate.

'Looking for treasures, are we?'

Steven almost jumps out of his skin. On the other side of the wall, outside the old shed, is Tony. He's not at all dressed for church but is wearing an overall. He has a black smear on his cheek.

'What are you doing here? Looking for a quiet place for a cuddle?' He grins, pleased with his own remark.

'Whatever it is, it's none of your business,' Isabella says.

'We can be here if we want to. You don't own this track.'

'Right you are, teacher's pet,' says Tony. 'But if you set one foot on our land I will call the dogs to say hello to you.'

'Come Steven, let's go,' Isabella says.

She's right. There's no point in seeking a confrontation with Tony, on his home ground. They've probably seen what there is to see. Isabella pulls him along, although he wishes she wouldn't. After a few steps he looks over his shoulder. Tony is still standing there, his eyes fixed on them as they walk back up the track to the main road.

7 A Fire in the Night

They walk back to the main road. They don't talk. Tony's threatening words are still ringing in Steven's ears. 'Looking for a place to cuddle?' What a stupid suggestion that was! Isabella and he are just friends, classmates. What business is it of Tony to mingle in their friendship? He wonders what Isabella is thinking, whether she is annoyed about that stupid remark too? What was the other thing that Tony had said? 'Looking for treasures?' What could Tony possibly know about their mission? Was he just guessing, having observed the two of them going up and down the track? It must have looked strange. How long had Tony been watching them?

'Look!' says Isabella, when they're back at the beginning of the track. 'They're building up the bonfire for tomorrow night. I'd forgotten it's Guy Fawkes night.'

How have they not noticed it on the way down? The enormous pile of timber on the hillside could hardly be missed. Every year on November the fifth the enormous fire is lit in the same location. On the hill above Bridge Farm it becomes an enormous beacon of light and flames, visible from miles around. The people of the village always gather on the bridge, right above the river, which is the best place to watch the spectacle.

'They build it higher every year,' he says. 'That pile will be the biggest fire they have ever had.'

They get on the main road and head back towards the bridge and the village, leaving the timber stack behind them. How long have they been out here? Half an hour perhaps? Forty-five minutes at the most.

'I don't think we're getting anywhere,' Isabella says. 'Maybe this isn't the Penny Cross we're looking for after all. It's a shame we didn't have more time to look around.'

'It has to be here,' he says, looking back down to the farm track. 'There was mining here and Thomas Carpenter was a mine captain. He must have crossed the river many times. That track is an old road and I guess the farm is pretty old too. There must be something we are overlooking, something we are just not seeing.'

'But what?' says Isabella.

'I don't know. If we are looking in the right place it can't be too difficult to work out what the giants and dwarfs are. If they aren't stones, they must be something else. Something eleven times big and five times small.'

He hears himself speak as if it's easy, as if it's like a simple crossword they have to solve. He almost convinces himself. Almost, because the reality is that they're stuck!

'We need to rethink,' he says after a while. How exactly he doesn't know. Neither does Isabella. They walk on in silence.

'Time for my practice,' Isabella says, when they're back at her house. Of course! She has her band rehearsal this afternoon.

'What time is your rehearsal?'

'Three o'clock.'

Steven says he will come to the rehearsal to take photos of the band. In a way it's a relief to have something else to think about.

Walking back to Greystone House he comes via Harewood Road again. He's not worried. Things have changed. He's no longer an easy target. His focus has changed. He and Isabella are on a mission. Even though they're stuck at the moment they have the TCA to work on. Tony and Andrew would not be able to outwit him any more, regardless of whether he's on his own or not. Anyway, bumping into them now is unlikely. Tony is at home at Bridge Farm, at least, he was there half an hour ago. Why had Tony suggested they were looking for treasures? Was he just calling their bluff?

As he arrives at the Old Copperhouse with his camera the band is already setting up. Joey is adjusting the height of the cymbals next to his bass drum, Marcus and Simon plug into their amplifiers. They look pretty professional. Joey looks very cool in his felt hat. He hasn't seen him wear that in school.

'How do you want to do this, man?' Joey asks, nodding at his camera.

He must admit he hasn't really thought about it. 'I'll first watch for a while,' he says. 'I'm sure I'll get some ideas for the photographs when I see you in action.'

'Cool,' says Joey. 'Let's give it a whirl then.'

As if by magic his classmates are on their stage spot. Simon strums the strings on his guitar once, waking up his instrument. Rebecca adjusts the mouthpiece of her clarinet and blows it through. Isabella snaps her fingers to set the beat: 'one, two, one, two, three, four'.

They are off. Joey takes the rhythm on his snare drum. Marcus adds bass notes. Simon and Rebecca come in.

Isabella brings the microphone up to her lips and the song lines come rolling out, first gently as a ship that floats away from the quay, then firmer as the ship is finding its course into the open water, whilst around it the waves are growing in size.

Steven can't believe what he's seeing. He's never heard Isabella like this before. He knows her as his school friend - clever, practical, positive. The person he sees now is someone else. She's electrifying, completely in control of the music around her, colouring her words as she sings them, sometimes even with her eyes closed. Her dark brown hair dances around her face and shoulders to the rhythm of the music. She's like a queen on stage. Joey, Marcus, Simon and Rebecca sometimes glance at one another briefly. They seem to know exactly what each one of them is doing. With no effort at all they push the boat forward over the water in complete harmony.

Isabella's first song is a slow number called 'Like a Dream'. Simon wrote the tune. It's their title song. The second song, 'Call me Up', is much faster. Isabella's stage personality changes with it. She has to work fast to get the words out in the right order and meanwhile she seems to challenge the imaginary audience to catch her out. Then they do a Beatles cover, followed by her favourite, 'Midnight Express'. It's hard to believe that all the different Isabellas he sees passing by are all the same Isabella, the same person with whom he had been surveying stones along a farm track this morning, only a few hours ago.

Steven suddenly remembers his camera. He's supposed to take photographs for the poster. He takes off the lens cap and zooms in on each of the players. He walks around them to frame them from different angles. He keeps on shooting, also in between numbers when they're discussing the sound or just make jokes about how the songs have come out.

'What do you think?' Simon asks when they take a break. Isabella hasn't looked at him while she was singing, but he can tell she's now waiting for his comment.

'I never realised,' he says. 'You are fantastic. I never thought you would be this good.'

'Cool man,' says Joey. Marcus grins. Rebecca adjusts her clarinet again.

'You're our first audience,' says Isabella.

'It's a premiere,' says Simon.

When they start playing again he gets an idea for the poster. He pictures a photograph of the band in front of an almost abstract image of the river, just waves, gradually fading. Above the photo of the band he wants cartoon-like drawings of instruments, symbols like Joey's hat or Marcus' scarf, floating like dreams on the water. Perhaps a majestic bird scanning the river underneath and right at the top the name of the band in bold, colourful letters: Blue River Dreams. He can use the close ups of each of the players in action either on the back of a flyer, or perhaps along the right hand side of the poster.

At the end of the rehearsal, he shows them the photographs on his camera and explains his idea for the poster.

'Sounds good to me,' says Simon.

'Photos on the front, I think,' says Isabella. 'Joey here wants to get famous on a lamppost.'

'Thanks, Bells,' Joey says.

Steven stays on with Isabella to help Joey pack away his drum kit.

'So, no more treasure hunting then?' Joey asks suddenly.

'What do you mean?' He's taken aback by Joey's direct question. This is the second time today that the word treasure is thrown at him.

'Isabella said something about you finding a key and getting an inheritance from an old miner. Sounded pretty exciting.'

'It was nothing,' he mumbles. He does his best to make it sound uninteresting. 'It was just a load of poems. Bit cryptic. Not worth the effort, really.'

'Cool,' Joey says.

'I only told him because TCA had ended,' Isabella says, when they walk back home together. 'I thought the papers were shredded and that the case was closed.'

She's right of course. He did reject the inheritance first of all and they both thought the papers were destroyed and that the case was closed. To be fair, they never actually agreed in words that the TCA should be a secret between them. At the same time he can't help feeling let down by Isabella letting others in on the case without him knowing.

'And Joey is a good friend,' Isabella adds to her defence.

'You're right,' he says. 'You couldn't know that the situation would change, that the papers were still there. We both didn't know.'

'I'm sure Joey is not that interested anyway. It's different when you haven't seen the testament papers yourself.'

'I guess that's true,' he says. He doesn't want to make an issue of all this. But he wonders if Joey could have told anybody else about it.

That evening Steven starts to work on designing the Blue River Dreams poster. He downloads the photos to his computer. He wants to work on it while the idea is still fresh in his mind. He wants to do something good for Isabella. He knows she must be feeling bad about having told Joey about the Thomas Carpenter business, even though he said it didn't matter and even though Joey didn't know now that the case had been re-opened. Really, was it so bad that Joey knew about it? He wants to work on the poster now, so that he can show Isabella his design soon and make up for being unnecessarily awkward earlier.

His mum brings him a drink and looks over his shoulder at the computer screen.

'That isn't homework, is it?'

'It's a poster I'm doing for Isabella,' he explains. 'It's Blue River Dreams, the band that she is singing with. They'll play at the Winter Fair at Oakendale Castle. Isabella asked me to do the graphics. They're really good.'

The next day Steven takes the poster design in with him to show to Isabella and the rest of the band. They all like it a lot, especially the different objects floating above the water. For the background he used a photograph of the river, which he took perhaps a year ago. He zoomed in on the water surface to create the abstract texture that he wanted. It is really quite dreamlike. Apart from a bit of tweaking and adding the relevant information about the band and the date and time of the event, the poster is pretty much ready for printing.

There's a kind of buzz in school because of Bonfire Night. In the village people start gathering on the square around seven o'clock. He comes down with his mum in the car. The evenings are too dark now for walking the distance between home and the village comfortably, let alone for walking back afterwards. Around half past seven everyone drifts towards the bridge, drinks in hands. Many people from the surrounding villages and from Callingfield have also come out to watch the spectacle. Steven spots Isabella in the crowd but she's moving away from him, heading for someone else. He loses sight of his mum and suddenly finds himself next to Joey. He's wearing his felt hat tonight. 'Hey, man,' he says.

'Hi Joey.'

'Thanks for working on that poster,' Joey says. 'It's a fabulous idea, all those floating things.'

'I'm glad you like it. When I watched you all play in the rehearsal, I got the idea straight away.'

'Cool.'

'Joey, you know you were asking me about this treasure, this inheritance that Isabella told you about?'

'What about it?' says Joey.

'I just wondered if you had mentioned it to anyone else?'

'Why, shouldn't I have? I thought it had come to

nothing.'

'Yes, that's right,' he says. 'It hasn't come to anything.' It's a lie, but he just feels that the less people know about the Thomas Carpenter affair, the better.

'It's just..., well, to be honest, I'd rather not tell too many others about it. It was a bit embarrassing, this treasure fantasy.'

'Sure,' Joey says. 'I may have mentioned it here and there. I thought it was a pretty cool thing. But since you ask, I will keep my mouth shut. No problem.'

Steven is about to ask to whom Joey had mentioned it, but at that moment a man at the front of the crowd raises his voice and the torch that he holds in his right hand.

'Citizens! Civilians of the United Kingdom! We have come here tonight to remember the fifth of November of the year 1605, when a wicked attempt to blow up the Houses of Parliament and kill our King, James I, was only narrowly avoided. We have gathered to honour the principles of our democracy, celebrate the justice of our laws, and demonstrate our determination that we shall not rest until any person who acts against our State shall be tried and punished. Tonight we remember the Gunpowder Plot, how it was foiled, and how the evil plotter, Guy Fawkes, got what he deserved.'

With these words the man is handed a second torch, which he also brings up over his head. Everyone falls silent. Hypnotised they watch the two torches burning bright orange in the dark night. Then, in one fluent movement, the speaker brings the two torches down to the ground. Immediately, on the other side of the river, two torches light up. It's quite a distance away, but in the torchlight the contours of the enormous pile of firewood are clearly visible. The distant torches come down too. They're held at the foot of the timber pile. Within a minute the flames take hold of the wood. It doesn't take long before the flames get a firmer grip on the timber. The yellow and orange light expands in width and height. The fire in the night quickly becomes an imposing beacon, casting its light over the river and the village. The crowd is no longer kept back by their torchbearer and spreads out along the bridge, finding the best places to watch the spectacular fire on the other side of the water.

Steven is mesmerised by the bright flames rising high up in the black night. Only yesterday morning he and Isabella were so close to the timber stacked up and waiting on the hillside. Now the stack has become this all-consuming fire. He notices the buildings of Bridge Farm glow warmly in the orange light. The old mine chimney at the back of the farm is like a dark finger pointing up to the night sky, and casting a long shadow towards the bridge and the village.

His heart almost stops. The chimney! It seems to be pointing at him, calling him. Could it be? Is this perhaps one of the giants on the road to Penny Cross? He looks again. The sharp shadow of the chimney falls straight over the track to Bridge Farm, right where the track curves alongside the river for its last hundred metres towards the farm. He has to go there! He has to go now.

Most people are still watching the burning pyre intensely, others have started commenting and chatting. He moves to the far side of the crowd. Away from the torches the night is darker and people appear as shadows. Steven looks to see if anyone is watching him. Then he steps out from the crowd into the dark and quickly heads to the other side of the river.

Very soon the night swallows him up. Everything is pitch black around him, but he knows where he's going. It doesn't take him long to reach the point where the track to Bridge Farm starts. 'The Road to Penny Cross' he says to himself as he goes down the track for the second time in two days. Although the ground is uneven, seeing where he's going is easy. His eyes are getting used to the dark and further down the track is lit up by the enormous fire in the field above. Before him the strong shadow of the mine chimney slices across the track like a knife. He runs the last two hundred metres to where that shadow hits the track. He doesn't bother this time observing the stones in the walls on either side for a pattern of bigger and smaller stones. He heads straight for his target. He's sure that's what the long chimney shadow is doing – helping him find the second stone.

He reaches the bend in the track. Here he's right in the middle between the bonfire on the hill and the crowd on the bridge, faintly lit in the distance. Can they see him here? Who cares, he doesn't have time to worry about it. He concentrates on the shadow at his feet, determined to understand what it is telling him.

At once he sees it. Where the shadow climbs up against the wall of stones on the left hand side it glides over a huge round stone in the wall, a stone almost like a mill wheel. Why didn't he and Isabella spot this one yesterday, when they were investigating by daylight? He steps closer and runs his hand over the stone. It is a rough stone but its surface is reasonably straight. In the centre it has a stump, sticking out as if it is the axle of a wheel. He closes his hand around it. As he tightens his grip he feels the stone cut into his fingers, but he also feels something moving. He presses his fingers even tighter, ignoring the cutting, and pulls. The stump comes away. He holds his breath when it comes out leaving a small dark opening in its place, just big enough to reach into with his hand. As he pushes his hand forward his fingers have a familiar sensation: a smooth, metal object, hidden in the stone and waiting to be revealed. He knows he has found the second stone and the secret contained within.

'Hey, who are you? What are you doing here?'

At the stone barn on the other side of the wall, where Tony had stood yesterday morning, a large man has appeared. He can't see his face clearly because of the light of the fire behind him, but he's pretty sure it's the farmer, Tony's dad. Behind him, coming down through the field more shadowy figures are approaching. They're all coming down from the fire higher up the hill. Without a doubt one of them is Tony.

'Nothing sir,' he says, pretending to be sheepishly caught out. But his mind is far from sheepish as he pulls his hand back and starts walking backwards.

'Wait!' the farmer shouts. 'What are you doing on this track in the dark?'

He has no intention of waiting. He turns around and starts running, back to the main road. He has the advantage. The farmer is on the other side of the wall and has no easy way of getting over it. He sees that Tony starts running too, through the field, heading for a cattle gate further on. As a result of looking sideways he loses his footing on the uneven track and falls, but he's down for a moment only. He continues running. Having to run through the muddy field on the other side Tony is in no way able to catch him out. He is soon back on the main road and he knows that he is safe, but he keeps on running back to the bridge until he's much closer to the people. Then he slows his pace, waits a few moments to get his breath back, before he slips back into the crowd as if he has been among the people all the time. Tucked away in his trouser pocket his right hand is safely holding the cylinder that he has taken from the second stone.

8 Two More Brains

'What I would like to know,' Miss Henderson says, 'is whether anybody here did not see the magnificent bonfire spectacle on Monday night?'

She looks around the classroom. Nobody raises an arm. Clearly all of them have watched the fire from the bridge or from somewhere else in the village. If any of them have accidently missed Guy Fawkes' Night, he or she is now wise enough not to admit to it.

'Perfect,' Miss Henderson says. 'That confirms beyond reasonable doubt that you are all deeply interested in history, which works out well, because history is on the agenda for today.'

Typical of her! Miss Henderson starts her lesson as if it's a pain, as if none of them would feel like doing it.

'So this Guy Fawkes character?' Miss Henderson asks. 'Was he a good or a bad person? Why do we still burn his effigy on the stake?'

Most of them agree that Guy Fawkes had been a bad person for trying to blow up Parliament and the English King and all, but there is also discussion about why he had made the attempt. Tony raises his arm.

'I don't care much, Miss, whether he was good or bad, but I did enjoy burning him.'

Most of the class laugh, of course. They all know that Tony was right there with his father on Bonfire Night and held the first burning torch to the pyre. Yesterday he was bragging about it all day long.

'Right,' Miss Henderson says. 'I'm pleased that Guy

Fawkes sparked your imagination Tony. And may I say well done? It must have been the biggest bonfire we have ever seen. Truly magnificent!'

Miss Henderson continues. 'What I find interesting,' she says, 'is that although this business with Guy Fawkes and the Gunpowder Plot happened more than four hundred years ago, which is a very long time, we still have a good picture of what actually went on that night. We have a fair amount of credible information from that time. We still have the Houses of Parliament and can go and see for ourselves where the gunpowder was stored and where Mr Fawkes was caught in the act of plotting. There are even eye witness statements, that tell us more or less what happened, or rather what could have happened, but didn't. After four centuries we can read history as if it was yesterday's newspaper and we can form our own opinion on who was right and who was wrong. Correct?'

They all nod, waiting to see where she is going with this.

'Well, today I would like to take you back a lot further in time,' she says. 'I would like to take you back at least one thousand years or more, back to the time of King Arthur, whom we discussed before. You could say that from that time we also have some newspaper clippings left. Unfortunately there aren't very many and the ones that we have are so old that they are difficult to read. Even if we decipher the news features of that time, it is difficult to believe that what we read is true. It's difficult to decide if the stories from that long ago are true stories, based on facts, or whether they are merely fantasies, penned down by an inspired scribe. So today I am going to treat you to the story of Sir Perceval and the Holy Grail. By the end I hope you can tell me whether his adventures really happened or whether they are nothing more than a cleverly made up story.'

She picks up an old-fashioned hardcover book from her desk, opens it where she has put a strip of paper between the pages and starts reading. She reads about Sir Perceval, one of King Arthur's Knights of the Round Table, who made a pledge to find the Holy Grail, the cup that was said to have collected the blood of Jesus when he was taken off the cross and was said to have mysterious powers. It was believed that the Holy Grail had been taken from the Holy Land to King Arthur's lands – England - but had somehow disappeared. Although many had tried to trace it, no one had ever found it. For Sir Perceval this was of course all the more reason to go after it. He made it his quest to find the Holy Grail and bring it to his King, whatever it might take. And so he travelled tirelessly, fighting evil on his way, wherever he found it. He fought with dragons that terrorised the people with fire and fear and he defeated Castle Lords who kept innocent princesses locked up in their towers.

'Towards the end of his life,' Miss Henderson concludes, 'as Sir Perceval lay dying from a mortal wound inflicted upon him by a masked, black knight, his many adventures passed before his eyes and he felt he had lived truthfully, and that he could die in peace. His only regret was never to have found the Holy Grail.'

A silence follows as Miss Henderson closes the book. She gives them time to let the story sink in. Then she pulls them back to reality and asks: 'So, a true story or not, this quest for the Holy Grail?'

'Not true!' says Rebecca. 'It's a great story, but if the Holy Grail was never found, how can we know that it really exists?'

'It could be true,' says Isabella. 'Maybe it just hasn't been found yet. Somebody must have seen it once. How else could it have ended up in a story?'

'Just because it's in a story, that doesn't mean it really exists,' says Alex. 'Someone could have just made it up.'

It's an intense debate. Most agree that without anyone ever having seen the Holy Grail it's hard to prove that Sir Perceval's quest was anything more than a good story, but the opinions remain divided. In the end what seems to matter most is whether you want to believe that it could be true, that Sir Perceval had really once roamed the earth chasing after the object he desired, or whether you feel it doesn't make much difference, because after all time has moved on and things are different now.

During the whole discussion Steven doesn't say anything. The story has stirred many thoughts in his mind. Whilst Miss Henderson was reading, he was constantly reminded of his own quest. Is he also chasing something that perhaps doesn't even exist? Could he, just like Perceval, be making all this effort without ever finding a reward at the end? He remembers the solicitor's long letter, encouraging him not to ignore Thomas Carpenter's words, but at least try to work out what they mean. They have already uncovered the meaning of two of his cryptic verses. Perhaps in any quest it matters more where you go and what you do, than whether you really find a treasure. Looking at it in this way, he comes back to the simple question he has asked Isabella before: What is there to lose?

Last Monday night, when he had made it back safely from Penny Cross, Steven knew exactly what he had to lose. With the silver capsule burning in his pocket and in his mind the triumph of solving the puzzle of the second stone, the Thomas Carpenter Affair was all that mattered to him. He desperately wanted to tell Isabella about his success and tried to find her in the crowd, but she had gone home already and his mum was waiting for him to go back to Greystone House.

As soon as his mum had driven their old Ford up the bumpy drive and they were back inside, he said he was tired and going to bed. He even rejected the hot chocolate his mum offered to make.

Alone in his room he took the new cylinder from his pocket and inspected it. It was almost identical to the first one he had found, although this one was smaller and more difficult to undo. After a bit of struggle he managed to take both halves of the cylinder apart. There was no key or object inside, only a rolled up piece of old paper. He unrolled it carefully and stretched it. He recognised the handwriting, the strongly accentuated swirls with which Thomas Carpenter had written a new cryptic puzzle. It said:

They Stand, They Guard, Take Heed
Around the Alabaster Skies
The Third Stone under Flying Foot
The Broken Man the One You Need

Contrasting thoughts went through his mind. He was excited by the new mysterious words promising a new adventure. He was also disappointed. Only an hour ago he had felt so victorious in having found the second stone and getting away with his prize while the Turners couldn't stop him. To find nothing inside the capsule now, other than a new riddle, seemed a poor reward for his success. A 'well done' from Mr Carpenter would have been nice. He turned over the scrap of paper, hoping to find any further messages or explanations, but the other side was completely blank. The new words were all he had, and no idea yet as to what they meant.

It was too late to phone Isabella. There was really not much else to do now. He brushed his teeth, got into his bed and read the new words over once more before he switched off the light. He lay in the dark with his eyes wide open and his mind in no way ready to shut down and rest. These words were more cryptic than before. They didn't even give any indication of where to look. Steven was pretty sure that all these words had to be code, that they really all meant something else, just as the giants and the dwarfs had done. Suddenly he realised that the secret of the second stone was not really solved. Thomas Carpenter's words had mentioned eleven giants and five dwarfs, but in the end it was just one gigantic chimney that had pointed to the location of the second stone. Where or what were all the others? Did it matter now? He realised that he had been lucky to find the second stone. Would he be as lucky again in the pursuit of this new one? And then, no doubt, there would be more stones with messages to find, if ever he would get to the last one. He definitely needed more luck to have any chance of succeeding. And he needed Isabella. He pictured himself telling her the next morning about the second stone, the shadow of the chimney, his getaway in the dark, and the new message. As the thoughts went round and round in his mind he finally fell asleep.

On Tuesday morning, as soon as he saw Isabella in the schoolyard, he had gone up to her.

'I have news,' he said, and with his eyes he indicated her to look down. He opened his hand to show her the silver capsule before he quickly closed it again and put the capsule back in his pocket. Isabella's eyes had grown big.

'How did you ....? Where ....?'

Before he had a chance to answer the school bell buzzed again. Any business other than school business would have to wait.

In class Isabella kept throwing meaningful looks in his direction, but she had to wait until lunchtime before he finally had a chance to tell her about his discovery the previous night. He told her how he had got away under the nose of Tony Turner and his father. They probably still didn't know why he had been there in the dark.

'Can I see it?' Isabella said. 'What was in it? Was there a new message?'

With so many others around them he didn't like to bring the capsule into full daylight, but he briefly showed her, before he put it back into his pocket. He took a writing pad as if he was showing her work he had done at home. In the writing pad he had copied the words from the third

TCA verse. This way Isabella could read them without having to act suspiciously.

'Does it make any sense to you?'

'Not immediately' Isabella said.

At that moment Tony Turner appeared, closely followed by Andrew. He quickly closed his note pad.

'I believe you have something that belongs to me,' Tony said. He stood right in front of him trying to stare him out with his cold blue eyes.

Steven didn't blink.

'What do you mean?'

'I know what you were doing last night on our track,' said Tony. 'Andrew told me all about it.'

'And what exactly might that be? What does Andrew know about anything?'

He had been in no way afraid. Tony and Andrew would never try anything against him in the schoolyard. He was fairly sure that Tony couldn't have seen that he took the capsule from the stone. Perhaps he had walked past the cavity in the stone this morning, but there are lots of stones with holes in them. He didn't believe that Tony would have noticed anything unusual.

'We know about your treasure from that miner,' Andrew said. 'Joey told me all about it.' Andrew's face was paler than Tony's. He was less direct. He acted as if he was the one in control, which made him even more vicious.

Isabella tightened, hearing them speak about the miner's treasure, but he was prepared. He knew from Joey that the secret had been talked about. Joey was into biking and so was Andrew. It was to be expected that Joey could have mentioned it to him. Andrew would have told Tony. That would explain why last Sunday morning Tony had used the word 'treasure'.

'You mustn't believe everything Joey says,' he said, as straight faced as he could. 'All that drumming he does has made him a bit light headed.'

Isabella had looked at him, not quite sure what to make of his reply and not quite believing how he had just insulted their mutual friend. He kept his face in line.

'Let me say this to you, teacher's pet,' Andrew said. 'Whether you are looking for a treasure or not, we are keeping a close eye on you.'

'If you set one more foot on our track,' Tony added, 'poking your nose around our farm, I will make sure you won't get away again.'

'It's not your track,' Steven said, 'and let me say this to you in return. Just try a little harder. Maybe one day you can be teacher's pet yourself.'

'Don't need to,' Tony said. 'I've got this.'

Tony made his hand into a fist and held it in front of his face. But Steven didn't flinch.

That had been Tuesday during school. At the end of the afternoon he had gone home with Isabella as usual, where he had finally been able to show her the capsule in full, and the scrap of paper with the four lines in Thomas Carpenter's handwriting.

'We were incredibly lucky to be looking for the second stone just as it happened to be Bonfire Night. I don't think I would have discovered it without that fire. But I still don't understand why eleven giants and five dwarfs.'

'Without the fire,' Isabella said, repeating his words.

'That's it! Of course, Bonfire Night, the fifth of November! You needed the bonfire to see the shadow cast by the chimney. November is the eleventh month of the year, and bonfire night the fifth day of November. Eleven giants and five dwarfs - that is what it must mean: eleven months and five days.'

'But how ....?' But he realised that Isabella had to be right. It made perfect sense. Thomas Carpenter must have known that an enormous fire was needed to make the chimney cast its shadow.

'But in that case,' he said, 'the bonfire for Guy Fawkes' Night must have always been lit in the same place. How could Mr Carpenter have known that so many years after his death, people would still be lighting the bonfire in that same spot on November the fifth?'

'Well, he probably never thought that it would take this long for someone to be curious enough to solve the words on his gravestone,' Isabella said. 'For someone to be clever enough to find the cylinder with his words, leading to the testament.'

'It almost makes you think he didn't want his riddles to be solved.'

He had been flattered that Isabella had just called him clever. Had it been anything other than luck to be knocked out against the gravestone and discover its secret?

'Why would he have gone to all that trouble of hiding his words and making a trail, if he didn't want anybody to uncover them one day?' Isabella said. 'Maybe he could look into the future? Maybe he knew that the bonfire would always be lit there on November the fifth.'

That was going too far for Steven, although he had to

admit that the date offered a good explanation for giants and dwarfs. 'At least we can now explain the full riddle,' he said. 'It makes sense.'

As to the meaning of the new words retrieved from the second stone, they had very little to go by. This time there wasn't even a place name, old or new, that at least gave some sense of direction. They both thought that the words 'They Stand, They Guard' could be a reference to something like a prison, but they had no idea why, or where there was or had been a prison. 'Around the Alabaster Skies' was even more confusing. How could someone stand guard around the skies? The internet wouldn't be much help this time. By the end of the afternoon they still had no plan of action to find the third stone.

Now it's Wednesday already. Miss Henderson has treated them to the fantastic story of Sir Perceval and his Holy Grail, which has left his mind in turmoil. How will he ever be able to find the third stone?

By the end of the school day Steven's mind is made up. 'Look Isabella,' he says, when they walk home together. 'About this third stone and the new words to find it... We're pretty much stuck, aren't we?'

Isabella hesitates. She doesn't know what he's going to say. Perhaps she thinks he might want to give up again. Not this time.

'I think we need some help. It was great that we found Mr Liddell, how you worked that out, and then, with a bit of guess work and lots of luck, how we found the second stone. But this new verse is even more cryptic. I think we need more brains this time.'

She seems relieved.

'Who are you thinking of?'

'I was thinking Joey. He already knows something about it. I thought it might be useful to get him on our side, if only to make him swear to secrecy. Do you think he would join us?'

'I'm sure he would,' she says. 'It would be great. Joey knows the area really well from all his mountain biking.'

'Great. Let's ask him.'

'What about my cousin, Sandy? Although she didn't know about Penny Cross, she does know a lot because of her job.'

'Can we trust her?'

'Definitely! I'm sure she would like to be involved. She loves doing something different.'

So they agree to extend their treasure hunting team with Joey and Sandy, if at least they are interested in coming on board.

The following day in school they take Joey aside. Steven has thought about how best to ask Joey. First tell him about the inheritance, the cryptic puzzles and the fact that the case has been re-opened, and then ask him to become part of the team? Or first make him swear to secrecy and then give him the story of what they had discovered so far - in case Joey wouldn't want to join them? Steven feels certain that Joey can be trusted, so he tells him up front that the TCA is on again and that he and Isabella need his help.

'Cool, man,' Joey says. 'A treasure hunt, I'm in. Honoured! What is our next move?'

He admires this in Joey, his ability to make up his mind on the spot. He has always looked up to Joey. It feels strange that now he's in the driving seat, asking Joey to step into his adventure. He tells him how the whole affair began in the cemetery. Joey whistles through his teeth. He knew Andrew and Tony from the biker's club. He hadn't known about them picking on Steven.

'It's important,' Steven says, 'for all of us, that we keep TCA to ourselves. Tony and Andrew have heard about the treasure, through no fault of yours, Joey, as you didn't know the case was still live. They don't know for certain that there could be a treasure. We need to keep it that way!'

'We have to be careful,' Isabella adds. 'They must have their suspicions, having seen us on the track to the farm. I think Tony was bluffing the day before yesterday in the schoolyard, but he did say they would keep an eye on you.'

'Three against two now,' Joey says. 'We're ahead.'

'Four,' Isabella says. 'We're going to ask my cousin Sandy too. She works at Oakendale Castle.'

On Saturday afternoon there is another band rehearsal. Isabella has arranged with Sandy that they can come to the National Trust office in the morning to print the posters. They agree to go all three to ask her if she's willing to join the team.

They leave their bikes at the ticket booth. The lady in the booth phones through to the main house and asks them to wait. It's a drizzly day. Despite the rain, the courtyard is full of visitors wanting to see the castle. Is this where the band will be performing? It's difficult to picture people in the courtyard stopping and listening. Is Isabella thinking the same? Will people stand in the winter cold to hear them play?

'I see that you've come with a whole committee for printing these posters.'

Steven had pictured Sandy with light coloured hair, but her hair is completely black. She is tall and slim and wears a bright red jacket over her dark skin. She radiates confidence. He is instantly sure that Sandy is able to analyse and solve any riddle that she's given, and that she would be a great addition to their team. He hopes she'll want to get involved. She's probably more than twice their age. Will she take them seriously?

'Come this way.' Sandy leads them through a side door, away from the stream of visitors, into a private part of the garden. They walk over a gravel path to the main house. Sandy pushes a series of numbers on a security keypad and opens a heavy door, decorated with a pattern of iron nails. They come into a spacious entrance hall, with a wide staircase in the middle.

'One of the pleasures of working for the National Trust!' Sandy says. 'You often have a castle for your office, although not always properly heated.' They follow her up the stairs to a room on the second floor where she has her desk and computer. The big new printer is next door.

'Let's have a look at this poster then,' Sandy says.

He takes a memory stick from his pocket and gives it to

her to plug into her computer. He directs her to the right file. The Blue River Dreams poster appears in full colours on the screen of Sandy's computer.

'This looks great! What a lovely poster! I'm in no doubt this will sell us tickets for the Winter Fair. How many shall we print?'

Isabella and Joey look at each other. Neither of them have thought about this yet.

'A hundred?' says Isabella.

'A thousand?' says Joey at the same time.

'I'm not sure there are that many poster places in the neighbourhood,' Sandy says. 'It would be expensive to print that many. Let's start with fifty and circulating those. We can print more if you run out.'

She clicks her computer mouse. The printer in the room next door wakes up.

Whilst the posters are pushed out from the machine one at a time, Isabella finds the courage to bring up the Thomas Carpenter Affair.

'Sandy, there is something else we wanted to ask you,' she says. 'Do you remember I asked you about Penny Cross, whether you knew a place by that name?'

Sandy nods.

'Well, we have discovered where it is. It turned out to be not far from here, on the river where Bridge Farm is. That used to be called Penny Cross.'

'That's interesting,' says Sandy. 'Well done for finding out! Was it something to do with a poetry project that you were working on?'

'Kind of,' Isabella says. 'But it's not really for school.'

'So what is it about then?'

Isabella looks at him.

'It is about an inheritance I've had,' Steven says. 'From a miner who used to live around here. It could be a fortune. We don't know, we first have to find it.'

Then he tells her the whole story. When he goes too fast Isabella adds explanations. At the end she says: 'The information we have to find the next stone is just too difficult. We need more help and we were wondering.....'

Sandy already knows what Isabella wants to ask.

'Can I see the papers?' she says. 'The testament and the messages you've found inside those cylinders?'

He has come prepared. He prefers to leave the papers in the security of Greystone House – he has started re-using the original wooden box for this – but he expected that Sandy would want to see evidence that their story is more than imagination. He takes the wooden box from his bag and opens it on Sandy's desk. All the papers are neatly inside.

Joey, who hasn't yet seen the real documents, whistles between his teeth. He's clearly impressed to see the adventure materialise in the old documents and handwriting. Sandy carefully takes the testament and studies it. She asks to see the latest verse, the four lines of the riddle that should lead them to finding the third stone. He shows her the scrap of paper and the words.

After a while she says: 'I am not sure about the broken man, but the first line makes me think of a place with a high wall. The alabaster in the second line is a kind of stone. You probably know this already. I think it is a translucent type of stone. Maybe that's why it says alabaster skies.'

'So do you....' Isabella starts. 'Do you want to be part of

our team?'

'Of course I do,' says Sandy. 'I wouldn't miss it for the world. A proper treasure hunt! That's a chance you don't get every day. And this one seems to be all around here, right up my street, so to speak.'

'Hurrah!' Isabella shouts.

'Thank you,' Steven says.

'So is there anything I need to do to become an official member of the posse?' Sandy asks. 'Do I need to sign anywhere in blood or swear on my life to adhere to the national secrecy act?'

'Keeping the secret,' Isabella confirms. 'We don't want everyone to know. There is too much at stake.'

Joey grins. Steven can't stop himself doing the same. He's going to like this.

9 The Manor House

'OK,' says Sandy, when everyone's excitement has calmed down. 'Let's get down to business. Going back to the word alabaster, I can't help thinking about Albaston, that village with the pub on the crossroads.'

Of course! Why hadn't he made that connection?

'I think that used to be called Alabaston. A 'ton' in a place name normally refers to 'town', so that would make this Alabast town. Could be worth checking out.'

'I often pass the pub there,' Joey says. 'There is a good bike trail that runs through the village.'

'Any high walls along your trail?' Sandy asks.

'Or a prison?' Isabella says.

'Haven't noticed,' says Joey. 'Actually, thinking about it, there is this big place. It looks pretty grim from the outside. I think it's called Albaston Manor. Has a big electric gate and all.'

'Rich people?' asks Sandy.

'Not the faintest idea! You don't get a look in. It's big and so is the wall around it. You can just about see the roof of the house behind it.'

Isabella says: 'I think we should investigate it. Why don't we go now? We have a couple of hours before our band practice.'

Steven nods. Sandy's suggestion seems possible. You would expect the riddle to give at least some indication of place. Otherwise nobody would have any idea about where to start looking. Albaston could definitely be a candidate.

Unfortunately Sandy can't go with them. She's on weekend duty and has to be at work until five. Joey has to get his drum kit, so it's down to Isabella and him to make the first reconnaissance to Albaston and check it out. Sandy takes them back to the ground floor. Isabella has forgotten the posters. She quickly runs back up to collect them from the print room.

It takes them twenty minutes to cycle to Albaston. The worst bit is back up the hill from Oakendale Castle.

'I think this is what Joey calls Granny Gear Territory,' he says. Isabella doesn't reply. She saves her breath for the climb. After the steep hill it gets easier. There's only the occasional drop and rise in the road. In Albaston they turn left at the pub and past the post box. As Joey said, the big walled house should be quite a way beyond the last house in the village, so they keep going.

After about a mile the high wall rises up on the right. The road is narrow here, making the wall look even taller. They cycle slowly past the entrance drive. The metal interweaving on the electric gates is too dense to see through, unless you would push your face right against it. At the end, as the road veers left, the wall actually bends to the right. There is a path alongside it. It's muddy and half overgrown. They put their bikes out of sight and continue their investigation on foot.

Steven soon realises there is little to investigate. The wall here is just as high, about two metres, making it impossible to look over it. They follow the muddy path along. After two hundred metres the wall bends to the right again. At no place is the brickwork lower or interrupted. The place is not keen to give any of its secrets away. From this side of the wall there is nothing more to discover, except that the Manor is indeed thoroughly closed off from the outside world. Had there been barbed wire on top of the wall, it really would have looked like a prison.

They turn around to go back to their bikes when Steven spots a tree with a thick branch growing over the wall.

'Look!' He points it out to Isabella. 'That could help us.'

'Worth a try,' she says.

'Best if you go up,' he says. 'You're lighter than me.'

He positions himself under the branch, his back against the bricks of the wall, and puts his hands together to form a step for Isabella. She places one foot in his hands. With one hand on his shoulder and the other on the wall, she pushes herself up far enough to reach the branch. She uses his other shoulder for her next step and pulls herself on to the wall.

'What can you see?'

Isabella is still taking in the picture. Albaston Manor definitely is a house of considerable size. Various annexes are connected to a central building, which has a big arched entrance. More impressive than the building even is the landscaped garden which surrounds the manor house on all sides. There's a kind of calmness throughout the garden, as if everything is in exactly the right place. The low hedges, the gravel paths, the pines and other trees that rise from the green lawns – it all seems in perfect harmony. She imagines how beautiful the gardens would look in spring and summer, when the flower borders will be full of colour. The house has tall windows on all sides. From every window you would be able to see out to the garden, but no further. Her eyes follow the wall to the far end of the garden. It really is unbroken on all sides. It's keeping the outside world out as much as it's keeping this amazing garden out of view from passers by.

Had anybody been in the garden, they would have spotted her easily, exposed on top of the wall, but fortunately the garden is deserted. No wait, are there some figures in the far corner? She squeezes her eyes to see better. The figures aren't moving. She realises that what she's looking at is a circle of stone statues, positioned symmetrically around a pond. She can't see from here what they look like, but she sees how the pond reflects the sky above, even on a cloudy, drizzly day like today. 'They Stand, They Guard,' she says to herself. 'Around the Alabaster Skies.' She has seen enough.

'I'm coming down.'

Holding on again to the branch of the tree, she lowers her foot until her toes rest on Steven's shoulder, before she drops the other foot down to the step of his hands.

'And?'

'This is it,' Isabella says. 'They stand, they guard! There are stone statues around a pond. The pond reflects the sky, that's how they can stand around the sky. This must be the place we are looking for.'

He wants to see for himself, so it's her turn to make a step with her hands. She can't hold his full weight quite as well. He manages to get his hand over the top of the wall and hoist himself up just enough to look over the wall and into the garden. In the far corner he sees the pond with the statues as Isabella described. His arms don't hold his weight any longer. He lets himself slide back down along the wall.

Isabella looks at him.

'Positive!' he says. 'This is the place we're looking for. We have to make a plan.'

'That will have to wait,' says Isabella. 'My rehearsal is in half an hour.'

So cycling back to Lower Callick leaves Steven no time to think. They have to hurry. Isabella hasn't brought her music. 'I will have to rely on knowing my lyrics,' she says. They agree that he will phone her in the evening to discuss what to do next.

Forty five minutes later he is back home at Greystone House. His mum makes him a sandwich and a cup of tea. He doesn't mention Albaston Manor, but tells her they've been to the National Trust to print the posters and he shows her a copy. Then he wants to get his chess set out to give him time to think, but his mum says she wants a word. Not a good sign, normally. Does she have suspicions? Does she know that he's not telling her everything?

'Steven, I haven't troubled you with this so far. It didn't seem fair so soon after your stay in hospital, but now I think it wouldn't be fair if I didn't tell you.'

She looks at him. He doesn't understand what she's talking about. Something about his operation? He has no idea what she wants to tell him. He waits for her to speak.

'About a week ago I had a letter from the bank,' she says.

'It's about our house and the mortgage. Do you know what a mortgage is?'

He nods. Of course he does.

'I would so much like not to have to worry you with this,' she says. 'The trouble is that I have difficulty keeping up with payments. I'm just not earning enough on my own to pay for it all. When your dad was still here it wasn't an issue, but on my own I'm struggling. I've had to make arrangements with the bank over the last few years, but now they're saying that I should sell up. They're saying we should live somewhere more suitable.'

This is not at all what he expected. Selling up? Surely that can't be true!

'I'm so sorry, Steven. I know how you love our house, how we both love living here. It hasn't been easy, not since your dad's accident, but I've always thought this is the right place for us. But now I'm running out of ideas. I just can't think how to make ends meet.'

He stares blankly at his mum, not knowing what to say. Does she really mean they have to move? Move away from Greystone House? He can't take it in, he refuses to believe it. 'But this is our house,' is all he manages to say.

'I know, darling, I know. It doesn't feel right to have to leave. But unless something changes, I just can't see a solution anymore. I would work all the time in the world if we could stay here, but I'm only human. Your operation was expensive too and now this letter from the bank.'

So now it was his fault! As if it had been his choice to go into hospital. His mum had been pushing for the operation herself, not him! He feels hurt, but he can tell that his mum is clutching at straws. She is desperate, he can see that. Perhaps the cost of his operation has contributed to the problems with the bank, but sooner or later it would have come to this. Sooner or later his mum would have run out of money.

'When do we have to move?'

'I'm not sure yet,' she says. 'The bank says three months. They are giving us three more months. They say that if nothing changes they'll want the the house on the market by February.'

Steven still gets his chess board out. What else can you do? He's not even hoping to concentrate on a game. He just hopes it might put some calmness back in his mind. Bad luck! Staring at the black and white pieces doesn't help a bit. Not living at Greystone House? This house is where he was born! This is where he belongs! He can't picture himself being anywhere else. If only he could do something. If only the fortune he's trying to find could be a real treasure. He has no idea. He doesn't even know if the seventh stone really exists. Right now it's just as unreal as the prospect of having to leave Greystone House in three months time.

Despite himself his thoughts drift back to Albaston Manor, earlier today. As far as he can tell the place seems to offer a promise. Perhaps the third stone will be there, around that pond. Asking Joey and Sandy to become fellow fortune hunters has been a good move. Between them they've come up with new information and at least some sense of direction. The big question now is how and when to get closer to that pond. The Manor House clearly is privately owned. Simply ringing the bell and asking for permission to have a look is probably not the best idea. The electric gates are not exactly an invitation. Could they climb over the wall where they stood today? It would leave a long distance to go through the garden towards the pond. It's not impossible, but doing it by daylight could be risky. They would be in full view. Better to go when it's dark. But how would they be able to see the third stone – if at least it's there? He remembers the broken man in the riddle. Maybe it's one of the statues. If so, maybe it would be easy to find the third stone, unless more of the statues turn out to be broken. Statues often are. Too many questions, too many possibilities! The Thomas Carpenter affair is like a game of chess. There are so many possibilities. What is his best next move?

Later that evening he phones Isabella. Steven doesn't say anything to her about what his mum's told him about having to move. She asked him not to, for now.

Isabella has thought about the house at Albaston too. After their rehearsal she discussed it with Joey and she also spoke to Sandy. They've all come to the same conclusion. The best time to go would be at dusk, with enough daylight still to see where to go, but not enough to draw attention. The best way into the garden – the only possible way it seems – is over the wall, using the tree branch. They can bring a torch and a rope to make it easier to get over the wall and to get out quickly should they need to.

It's a plan and they agree they should strike when the iron is hot. Tomorrow will be the day, around four in the afternoon. Sandy will join them straight after work.

Sunday morning creeps by incredibly slowly. All day long Steven feels a strange tension through his body. One moment he's thinking about Albaston Manor, the next moment about Greystone house and having to move out. In three month's time! Where will they go? It makes him feel cross. Why isn't his father here? He died four years ago. Why? Why couldn't he have been more careful on his motorbike? He's ashamed to think like that, but he can't stop the thought. Then this inheritance. Why couldn't this Thomas Carpenter have left him something of value, something to pay off the banks? That would have been so much more useful than all this mystery.

His mind is going over their plans again. With a bit of luck perhaps later today they will be another step closer to the seventh stone. He knows they're planning to break the law. Although they won't exactly be breaking into someone's house, it is still someone's property. What if the owner sees them? The second stone on the road to Penny Cross was hidden under Tony Turner's nose, but at least it was on a public road. Now they have to enter into a private garden where visitors are definitely not welcome. He wonders if Albaston Manor has always been a private property. How would Thomas Carpenter have had access to the garden with its statues around the pond?

As soon as he starts thinking about that, he starts to doubt seriously whether they're looking in the right place at all. Suddenly it seems very unlikely that they will find anything other than a pond with garden ornaments. He knows he has to push these thoughts out of his head. There is no plan B. They have to take the risk and find out.

Steven meets Isabella at a quarter to four at the railway crossing. They're both on their bikes. He has told his mother he's doing schoolwork with Isabella at her house and will be back home at six o'clock. Isabella has told her mum the opposite, that she was going to work with Steven at Greystone House. White lies to keep the TCA a secret.

Joey is already there when they arrive at Albaston Manor. His bike leans against the wall and Joey is standing on the saddle, looking over the wall into the garden. He jumps off when he sees them. He isn't wearing his felt hat today, but instead a black woolly one that makes him look like a serious crime professional. Isabella and he also wear dark clothes. As much as possible they need to merge with the darkening afternoon.

They place their bikes further along the track, in the shadows of the trees. He thinks that one of them should remain on this side of the wall as a lookout. Joey volunteers.

'You two have been in this game longer than I have,' he says. 'You should bring back our bounty.' He demonstrates a short sharp whistle that he will use to alert them to danger if he sees anyone go in through the main gate.

The three of them look at one another.

'All set?' Joey and Isabella nod.

This time it's Joey who positions himself with his back against the wall and creates the step-up with his hands. Joey is taller than he or Isabella, which makes it easier to reach the branch and pull themselves on top of the wall.

Steven goes first. He has brought a rope ladder, which he improvised last night. He slings it over the branch, letting it hang down on the other side of the wall. When it's securely in place he climbs down and takes shelter behind a large shrub, freeing up the route over the wall for Isabella. Hardly a minute later she joins him. Then they are both in the garden of Albaston Manor.

The garden is as deserted as it was yesterday. It looks more shadowy now, in the fading light. The circumstances are in their favour. Steven observes that some of the rooms in the house are lit. There must be people inside. But the house is a good hundred metres away from where they are and there are plenty of shrubs and hedges to give them cover. They start moving in the direction of the pond. He guesses it's about four hundred metres away, not far to go if you can walk freely, but they shouldn't take risks and keep checking if all is still clear before they move to a next point of cover. Gradually they get closer to their target. Nearer to the pond there are more trees and shrubs. It's not difficult to find a place where they have a good view of the pond and the statues around it, but can't be seen from the house.

The pond is a perfect circle. The water surface is completely still. Even at this time of day the pond clearly and calmly reflects the expanse above it. 'Alabaster Skies,' he says to himself. The quiet spectacle couldn't be described more accurately.

Twelve stone statues surround the pond. They're more than life size and anchored on stone plinths. They have different poses and look old and weathered. They are positioned around the water with equal distances between them and enhance the perfect circle of the pond like the numbers on a clock. The whole scene fits the description in the riddle perfectly. Steven has little doubt now that this must be the location of the third stone. As if Isabella has read his mind she says: 'So how do we work out where it is?'

From the other side of the wall Joey follows Isabella's and Steven's progress through the garden, standing on the saddle of his bike. As they get further away it's more difficult to keep track of them in the fading light. Rather than stay put in his place under the tree he decides he'll be more useful closer to the main entrance, to make sure all is quiet there. He walks to the front of the walled garden. There's no need here to keep under cover. After all, he is on a public road and there's nothing illegal about him walking here. He passes the electric gate, still firmly closed, and walks along the wall at the other side of the garden. At this end he should be closer to where Steven and Isabella will be by now. Maybe he can find another place to raise himself up and look over the wall into the garden? Perhaps there is a good viewpoint further along, where the road moves away from the wall?

As he follows the wall to the left he suddenly sees a small ladder leaning against the wall. He goes towards it. Then he spots the three bikes lying in the grass, one of which he recognises. It's Andrew's.

'There are twelve statues,' Steven says. 'It looks as if altogether, pond and statues, this is some kind of clock. We have to work out which one is number three.'

'Easier said than done,' says Isabella. 'To know which one is the third you first need to work out who is number twelve.'

'Wait! The Broken Man! We need to look for one that is broken. That is what the riddle says.'

'We have to get up closer,' says Isabella.

In their desire to find the third stone they step closer to the statues. They have to put themselves more in view of the house. There is no other way. Fortunately the dusk gives almost full cover. Isabella goes along the left side of the pond. He takes the right side.

Some of the statues have muscular bodies, others are carved with drape-like clothes. They all look proud and powerful, as if they're invincible. Clearly they aren't, because a lot of them are damaged. They look weathered, their faces worn away and some have hands or even an arm missing. He looks for other signs on the statues and on the plinths as well, hoping to spot something sticking out, something that could indicate the hiding place for a silver capsule.

They both reach the opposite side of the pond. He's about to ask Isabella if she has discovered anything when suddenly they hear a trumpet. They freeze in their place. Ten steps away from them there's a man. He sits in a wheelchair parked on the cobbled terrace on that side of the pond. He has started playing a melody on his trumpet whilst looking straight at them. They had been concentrating so much on the statues that they hadn't noticed him. He must have been there all that time.

The man stops playing and rests the trumpet in his lap.

'Should I raise the alarm or have you two simply lost

your way and ended up here by accident?'

Steven doesn't answer, neither does Isabella.

'Something tells me,' the man says, 'that you have not come with malicious intent.' His face is wrinkled and weathered like the statues, and his eyes don't look too friendly, whatever he says.

'Don't worry,' he says. 'I can't do you much harm in this chair and I haven't been drinking, so all is fine. Judging by your behaviour around that pond I am getting the impression you've come looking for something. Perhaps I can help?'

Isabella seems to have recovered from the initial shock.

'What is this place?' she asks.

'Ah, I see,' says the man. 'No answers! Questions instead! Fair enough, I suppose. If you really have lost your way, you want to find out where you are, don't you?'

The man looks at them again, piercingly. He must know that they aren't really lost. He adjusts his seating position in the chair, lifting first one leg for a few seconds and then the other.

'This place,' he says, 'Albaston Manor - I'm sure you know that's what it's called - is a rehab centre. Poor sods like me come here to try to kick the habit in the tranquillity of these beautiful gardens.'

'Rehab centre?' Isabella repeats.

'That's right, pretty face,' the man says. 'Rehab centre! For old rockers like me, who find it difficult to stay off the bottle. Or drugs. Don't worry about it. You're too young for all that. Let's just say that we're here trying to be good again.'

'It's like a prison,' Isabella says.

'Not far off,' says the man, 'although all residents come here voluntarily. They want to keep us in of course. They want to keep us from the outside world. It's a private matter, you see. The big wall around the garden normally does a pretty good job keeping us on the inside and keeping intruders out. But it clearly hasn't stopped you from entering, so you must have an urgent reason to be on this side. I think it's time now that you should give me some answers. What is all this business about stones and clocks?'

Steven looks at Isabella. What does she think? After their initial fright it now seems clear that the man isn't planning to raise the alarm. His trumpet playing hasn't attracted attention from anyone else. They could run if they need to. The man would never be able to move fast in his wheelchair over the cobbles. He weighs his options and decides to trust him.

'We are looking for something,' he says. 'We are looking for a stone.'

'There are stones all over the place,' the man says. 'What is so special about this one, that you come looking for it in the dark?'

How much should he give away? He suddenly takes a decision. Something tells him that despite his rugged looks and piercing eyes, despite his demanding questions, this man is no enemy.

'It's a stone from an old riddle,' he says. It's the third stone. We think it must be somewhere here.'

'I see,' said the man. 'Treasure hunters! That is why you come trespassing at night.'

Trespassing? Has he made a mistake? Has he now said

too much? Is the man not as friendly as he sounds? No. It's just a word. Of course they're trespassing. The man is right.

'So why is this third stone so important? Is the treasure buried underneath?'

It's impossible to hold back now. Steven feels he wants to tell the man everything. 'Probably not,' he says. 'We are really looking for the seventh stone. It is all part of a bigger thing, something I have inherited from an old miner, but we have to find it first.'

'We think that the third stone will give us another clue,' Isabella adds. 'We hope there will be a coded message inside. A small verse.'

Were they stupid to trust this man and tell him everything? If they were, it's too late now. Somehow their whole secret mission has just come spilling out. The man in the wheelchair appears to be friendly, he could be on their side. A short whistle sounds in the distance. He waits for what the man will say. So does Isabella.

'This is terribly exciting,' says the man. 'What makes you think that this is the place, that this third stone should be here, in this godforsaken garden of alcohol abusers?'

'The riddle talks about this pond and the statues. At least we think it's this place.'

'Interesting,' says the man. 'I feel honoured that you so readily share all this information with me. Would you perhaps tell me what the riddle is, so that I can help you decode it? By the way, it's James. Most people call me Jimmy. And who do I have the pleasure of speaking to?'

'Isabella and Steven,' says Isabella. She looks at him to see if he feels the same. He nods. Then Isabella recites

the four lines of the riddle to the man in the wheelchair
- James, Jimmy. It feels easier now that they know his
name. They Stand, They Guard, Take Heed, Around the
Alabaster Skies. The Third Stone under Flying Foot. The
Broken Man the One You Need.

'Very interesting lines,' says Jimmy. 'Would make a good
song.' He sits quietly in his chair, thinking and not paying
much attention to them. After a while he speaks again.

'I can see where you're coming from,' he says, 'thinking
that those first lines refer to this place here. Alabaster is a
bit of a give away. And the statues make sense of course.
Lots of them are damaged, but perhaps that doesn't
matter. The house is full of damaged characters anyway.
But which of them is the third one?'

'We think the statues around the pond look like a clock,
because there are twelve of them,' Steven says. 'We thought
that if we could work out how they are positioned, we
would know which one is twelve o'clock and which of
them is at three o'clock.'

'I see,' says Jimmy. 'That's why you were discussing
clocks. But didn't you say there were seven stones? Is the
one you are looking for here the third of seven, or the
third of twelve, if you know what I mean?'

No, he doesn't completely follow Jimmy's reasoning.
Does he mean that the position of the statues around the
pond is not important?

'If you ask me,' Jimmy says, 'the significant words here
are 'Flying Foot'. Have you asked yourselves what these
statues are?'

He hasn't.

'They are all statues of gods, from the classic times -

Roman and Greek mythology. I don't know how old they are. They must have seen better days. I wonder if one of these gods might have been famous for being very fast. For having flying feet, so to speak.'

Jimmy looks at them intensely.

'My problem,' he says, 'apart from the drinking issue, is that I didn't pay enough attention in school. The only one I recognise is this one here, Aphrodite, the goddess of love and beauty, although not so pretty anymore. You see how she rests her foot on a seashell? It was said that she was born from the ocean.'

Steven steps closer to the statue that Jimmy points at. On the plinth under her feet is a worn down lump of stone, still recognisable as a big shell.

Isabella hasn't moved.

'Hermes!' she shouts. 'Hermes was the god of travellers, and the messenger of the gods. He is normally pictured with a winged sandal.'

Steven looks at her. How does she know? Why didn't he know this? They focus again on the statues. He and Isabella go around the pond again, inspecting the feet and footwear of all the statues. Jimmy stays where he is.

'This one,' Isabella calls out. He runs over to her. The statue looks like someone striding. Once he must have had a staff in his hand, but that has been broken off. His right foot is slightly in front and leaning on a lump of rock. On the sandals on his feet they can just make out, very faintly, a carved line that looks like a wing.

He inspects the rock on which Hermes' carved foot rests. It doesn't take him long to spot a stub sticking out at the back of it. He needs no further instruction. His hand closes around the stub. With a short pull it comes out and a cavity appears. Immediately he sees the silver capsule that they've been looking for. It's here, safely in its place. He takes it out and holds it up in the air to show Isabella and Jimmy that he has found it.

'I've got it!'

At that moment everything happens at once. Three figures jump out from the shrubs behind them and leap forward.

'I'll have that,' one of them says. He snatches the capsule from Steven's hand. It's Andrew. Andrew holds the capsule above his head. Steven pulls at his arm to reach it, but Andrew is too tall and strong. So are the other two boys. Tony is one of them. Of course! He pushes Isabella towards the edge of the water.

'Get off! What are you doing?' she shouts.

Neither Tony nor the other boy bother responding. They simply push her further back, until she has no space left behind her.

'Get off me,' Isabella shouts again. Tony pushes her again until she slips and falls backwards into the pond.

Steven tries again to reach Andrew's closed hand above him. He pulls at Andrew's arm and clothes with all his force. He can't reach the capsule. Suddenly Andrew launches out with his other hand and punches him in his stomach. He folds double on the pain, gasping for breath. But Tony is now also on him. Tony launches his fist and whacks him right in his face. A sharp pain slices through his head. He loses balance and also falls into the pond.

'Serves you right,' says Tony.

'What about the old man?' the third boy says.

'Leave him,' says Andrew. 'He's helpless anyway. We've got what we came for.'

Without giving them a second glance they turn around and disappear into the garden.

After Joey has given his warning whistle he climbs on the ladder and over the wall. The situation has changed. Andrew and two mates must have gone into the garden. The best thing he can do now is go in himself to warn Steven and Isabella, if he's not too late already. He is halfway between the wall and the pond, when he sees Andrew, Tony and Keith – he recognises him from the bikers club – coming in his direction.

They look at him aggressively but they don't stop. 'Whose side are you on, mate?' says Andrew as they pass. Joey hurries towards the pond. When he arrives there, Isabella and Steven stand dripping on the edge of the water. Steven's face is bloodied. He doesn't have to ask what has happened. Never has he seen Steven look so angry, or Isabella so miserable.

'They t-took it,' Steven says. He looks to all sides, working out what to do, in which direction to steam off his frustration. Joey suddenly notices the man in the wheelchair.

'Seems you are not the only ones on a treasure hunt,' the man says.

'We found the third stone,' Steven says. 'We f-found the capsule, but we've lost it to those ...!' He doesn't finish his sentence. He tries to be strong and not cry, but the frustration and desperation rise up from his stomach. He isn't able to say any more.

10 The Broken Man

'Look,' says Jimmy. 'There's not much more we can do right now.'

They're all in a pretty miserable mood.

'Do you know those boys?'

'They're in our class,' says Isabella.

'Andrew and Tony,' says Joey. 'The other one is Keith. I know him from the Bikers Club.'

'Is there any chance we can get this capsule back from them?'

Steven shakes his head. Isabella and Joey say nothing.

'Still, all might not be lost,' says Jimmy. 'If there is one thing I have learned in life, it's that getting a door in your face is not always a bad thing. It makes you look in other directions.'

What does he mean? Steven doesn't understand. Surely there's no other direction than finding the next stone? They need the capsule with the message. Without the message they don't stand a chance.

Jimmy continues. 'First things first! You two must get yourselves into dry clothes. And you need to get your face cleaned up. Are you alright?'

He nods.

'It's getting too dark now, but I think we should have a further chat about all this. I may have an idea.'

Jimmy takes a card from his pocket and hands it to him.

'Give me a call sometime.'

Steven takes the card but he doesn't have anywhere to

put it in his wet clothes, so he gives it to Joey.

'We'd b-better go,' he says. He looks around to the route back through the garden.

'You better had,' says Jimmy. 'I should go too.' He moves his wheelchair around, the trumpet lying in his lap.

'Thanks anyway,' says Isabella.

Jimmy already has his back turned to them and starts to make his way to the Manor House. The three of them head back to the other end of the garden. They don't worry anymore about being seen. It's completely dark, although the house is now lit up, spreading an orange glow over the darkened lawns.

Sandy is waiting for them on the other side of the wall. The lights of her motorbike are switched on, making it easier for the three to lower themselves back down from the tree branch over the wall.

'Any result?' She notices their wet clothes, and the gloomy looks on their faces. Isabella tells her what happened.

'That's bad,' Sandy says.

Steven suddenly feels the cold on his wet clothes. Being somewhere warm is all he wants now. They decide to go to Isabella's home. Joey has to go the other way, but Sandy comes along. They cycle fast, trying to ignore the cold. Sandy keeps just ahead of them on her motorbike. The prospect of the Italian warmth of Isabella's home pushes him along, just as much as the wish to get away from their misfortune in Albaston Manor's gardens.

'Whatever has happened to you? How did you get into

this state, the both of you?'

Isabella's mum is obviously shocked when they to step inside, their clothes wet and dirty.

'We fell into a pond, mum,' says Isabella. 'I need some dry clothes.'

Isabella's mother looks suspicious. She will surely want to know more. For now she doesn't ask any further questions. Fortunately.

'Come into the kitchen,' she says. 'The Aga will warm you up.'

She get Steven a blanket and throws it around his shoulders. Isabella goes upstairs to change. When she comes back down in clean trousers and a big woolly jumper the kitchen is filled with the smell of the tomato soup warming on the stove.

'So who is going to tell me che cosa is going on? I thought you were doing school work!'

Isabella's statement that they have fallen into a pond wasn't enough for her mum. It is getting more difficult to keep the TCA a secret. How can they explain that they were kicked into the water? But before either of them can speak, Sandy does.

'They were pushed into the pond by boys from school,' she says.

Isabella's mum looks at Sandy. She must be wondering how she is involved in this.

'Why? What pond?'

'In Albaston,' Sandy explains. 'We worked out that's where the third stone should be.'

'What third stone? Who are these boys?'

OK! So Sandy hasn't realised that Isabella's mum doesn't

138

know about the treasure hunt.

'We are looking for a fortune, mum,' Isabella says. 'It's Steven's. It all started after he had been in hospital. But we have to find it first.'

Isabella's mum looks even more puzzled after this. She observes the three of them. Then she turns around to the cooker to take the soup of the heat and pour them each a bowl full.

'That doesn't make much senso,' she says. 'You need to explain better.'

Steven does. Sitting in Mrs Carter's kitchen, the blanket over his shoulders and a bowl of hot tomato soup in his lap, he tells her everything that has happened up until this miserable afternoon at Albaston Manor. He doesn't enjoy telling it, at least not the end. At the end they have nothing.

The other frustating thing is that he has difficulty finding the words. He is getting stuck sometimes. His earlier frustration and desperation turns to anger. He is furious with their attackers and even angrier with himself. He should have been more alert! He should have expected the attack. OK, Joey was looking out, but Joey couldn't see the attackers on the other side of the garden. How did Tony and Andrew know about Albaston Manor anyway? Had they already been there on Saturday? Had they seen Isabella and him looking over the wall the first time?

'So who are these ragazzi, these boys?' Isabella's mum says. 'Must we call the polizia? You say they are in your school. I will speak to them.'

'Best not,' Steven says. Mothers always seem to think that things can be resolved by the police, or by a telephone call. 'It's like the first t-time I was attacked.' It happens again. Has his stutter come back? The blow to his face? He ignores it.

'They don't have any e-evidence. They will just d-deny it.'

As he says this he realises that this time they do have witnesses. Jimmy and Joey were there. But Jimmy might not want to speak to the police. Besides, they themselves climbed over a wall and trespassed into a garden. The police would want an explanation for that.

'We need to keep it secret,' he says. 'If we tell the real story, nobody will believe it.'

'Maybe all is not lost,' Isabella says. 'Tony and Andrew are too stupid. If the capsule has a message inside, they won't be able to work out what it means. We can steal it back.'

'I'm not sure,' Steven says. 'They're not as stupid as we think. They followed us to Albaston Manor. Somehow they must have known what we were doing there.'

'Perhaps I can do something?' says Sandy. 'They don't know me. Perhaps I can find out from them what they took from you?'

How exactly? He can't imagine how Sandy talking to Andrew or Tony could make a difference. Tony had warned him about using his fists. He hadn't been bluffing. Talking to him won't do any good. The information he needs is in the hands of the worst persons imaginable. If only he could have had a glimpse of the message hidden in the third stone. How could he have been so careless? The failure of it weighs him down like a stone. His mood turns dark and miserable. What's the point?

When Steven finally gets home, later than his mum expected, he tells her everything. Now that Isabella's mother knows about TCA, his own mum should also be put in the picture. He is worried about more stuttering, but it doesn't happen now. Perhaps it was just chance. He's calmer again. To his relief his mother doesn't want to phone the police this time. She doesn't suggest that what he tells her is just his imagination or that he should forget about it. He was right. She must have suspected that something was going on. Of course! Did he think she was blind? She asks to see the silver cylinders and the testament. It surprises him. She has enough on her own mind, with the mortgage problems and all that. But she studies the papers carefully and reads the testament and the letter of the solicitor.

'Mr Liddell is right,' she says when she has finished reading. 'It may lead to nothing, but words shouldn't be ignored.'

'Dried out nicely?'

Tony and Andrew are waiting for him at the school gate. Steven doesn't expect such immediate and open confrontation. He looks at them, he looks them straight in the face, but he doesn't say a word. They're not worth it. He walks on to join Isabella and Joey.

In the lunch break Tony and Andrew are back. Clearly they are desperately keen to rub in their victory even more.

'So how will you find your fortune now?' Andrew says. He bends forward and puts the smile on his ugly face right in front of him. Steven keeps his cool.

'What fortune?'

'Mustn't play stupid with us, teacher's pet,' Andrew says. 'We know all about your plans, your so called inheritance from Mr Carpenter. After all we introduced you to him in the first place, down there in the graveyard. Fortune by the Seventh Stone - sounds good to me!'

'After what Joey told us, we had a look ourselves,' says Tony. 'So we checked out what you and your girlfriend were up to on Sunday morning in the churchyard. Showing her your secrets.'

'Much worse,' said Andrew. 'Teacher's pet here was stealing silver treasures from an innocent man's grave. Not so very nice, is it? Not very decent.'

'I didn't steal anything!' he says. 'You did! What you took from me yesterday belongs to me. You have no right. Give it back!'

'No idea what you're talking about,' says Andrew. 'Did we take anything yesterday? We played football, didn't we?'

'How did you know about Albaston?' says Joey.

'Just keeping our ear to the ground, mate. You told us yourself about the fortune. We felt it was worth keeping an eye on further developments. All we had to do was just follow these two love birds to the spot.'

'Was easy,' Tony says. 'They only had eyes for each other.'

He makes a kissing sound with his lips. Stupid idiot!

'We're not love birds,' Isabella says angrily.

Steven ignores Tony. 'What was inside?' he says.

'I'm sure you would like to know,' Andrew says. 'You don't really think we're going to tell you, do you? Our turn now for a bit of treasure hunting.'

'It's not your treasure, man,' says Joey. He's getting really angry too.

'It is now,' says Andrew, 'and as I told you yesterday, you'd better think carefully about whose side you are on.'

'Not yours, man,' Joey shouts back, 'now that I know what you're about.'

'Your choice, mate,' says Andrew. 'Your choice completely. If you don't want to be my friend, that's fine with me. I always thought you were a bit out of your depth on your little bike.'

Isabella butts in. 'They'll never be able to work it out,' she says. 'They don't have the brains.'

'I wouldn't be so sure, love bird. Maybe we already know where to find this next stone.'

'Maybe we already know,' Tony repeats. 'Maybe we've already found it.'

They turn around, visibly pleased with themselves, and laugh loudly.

'What are we going to do now?' Isabella asks.

'Tony is bluffing,' says Joey. 'They can't have found anything yet.'

'Maybe they don't even have the words to find the fourth stone,' says Isabella.

Wishful thinking. It's unlikely that Tony and Andrew haven't read the words, which he so desperately needs to see.

'We should work on Tony', says Joey. 'I think he could give something away, if we can talk to him alone.'

'Sandy will help us,' says Isabella.

Not much chance, but despite how he felt yesterday,

Steven doesn't want to give up now. If anything, this confrontation has made him more determined.

'Will you ask Sandy?' he says to Isabella. 'If they have any information about the fourth stone, they won't be able to work it out just like that. Maybe that will win us some time.'

Andrew's and Tony's teasing has definitely woken up his anger. He is not going to give up, not yet. He'll fight for his fortune.

'We also need to phone Jimmy,' he says. 'He said he might help us. He helped us in the garden.'

Joey pulls Jimmy's card from his pocket. It says 'James Grant - Rocker' and gives a mobile telephone number.

'Let's phone him this afternoon,' Steven says.

Back at Isabella's house after school Steven feels nervous while he waits for the call to connect.

'Jimmy Grant speaking.'

'Mr Grant, it's Steven. You said we could call you.'

'I'm glad you did. I'm glad you're phoning me now. Time and tide wait for no man.'

Steven doesn't know why Jimmy says this.

'You said you could help us.'

'Perhaps, perhaps,' says Jimmy. 'I think I have something for you. You must come and see me. I like your story. I need to know more.'

They arrange to go back to Albaston Manor after school. Steven is not sure that Jimmy will be able to help them. Jimmy said he had something for him. On the phone he got the feeling that Jimmy wanted to know more for his own interest, rather than having practical help to offer. Maybe he thought that all that had happened at the pond and before was just a good story to entertain him for a while. But as things stand there's nothing more to lose. Steven can't deny that yesterday afternoon Jimmy was at least sympathetic to their search.

At four o'clock they're all back at Albaston Manor, Sandy as well. No need to climb over the wall this time. Joey pushes the bell button and waits to speak into the microphone grid, but he doesn't have to. Without a word the enormous electric gates that seal off the estate separate, slowly and soundlessly. They take their bikes and Sandy's motorbike into the drive. Jimmy in his wheelchair waits for them on the paved area outside the main doors.

'It's good of you to come.' His eyes take in Sandy. 'And you have brought reinforcements?'

'This is Sandy, my cousin,' says Isabella. 'She's part of the team.'

'Perfect! Team spirit is what is required. Come inside, I have ordered tea.'

Jimmy turns the handle of the enormous manor house door and moves his wheelchair through. They follow him in.

On the inside Albaston Manor is even more impressive than from the outside. The entrance hall is spacious with high, decorated ceilings like in Oakendale Castle. There is an enormous staircase in the middle of the entrance hall. The hall has marble floors with antique tables and bookcases around the walls.

'Not much use to me,' Jimmy mutters, pointing at the

staircase, 'but the floors here are great when you're on wheels.'

He takes them to a lounge on the right hand side. This room is also full of antiques and has big paintings on the walls. They sit down on delicate looking sofas with faded furnishings. He notices the gardens through the windows. This room has a direct view of the pond and the statues around it.

'Well, here we are,' says Jimmy when they all sit down. 'I do hope you all like herbal tea? It is the only thing I drink when I am here.'

A girl in a light green uniform comes in with a tray of cups and a teapot.

'Are you staying here for a holiday?' Sandy asks.

'Ha!' Jimmy laughs. 'I'm not so sure about that. Your friends haven't been gossiping about me, then? No, I'm here to be sorted out. I need a little help with my drinking problem.'

'I was told you're a musician,' says Sandy.

'I was a musician,' Jimmy says, 'and a good one too. Then I started drinking. Now I'm here.'

Joey's face suddenly turns bright pink. 'Were you a singer in a band?' he asks.

He falls over his words. All Joey's usual coolness is gone.

'Yep,' says Jimmy. 'Front man, me! You may have heard of our band. We were pretty good. But then I had the accident and it was all over. Nobody wants to scream at a rocker in a wheelchair on stage.'

'Isabella is a singer too!' Steven says. She blushes as he

says it.

'What happened?' Sandy asks.

'It was shameful,' Jimmy says. 'Stupid and shameful. I walked away drunk from a gig. Walked on to the road without looking and was scooped up straight away by a lorry. Not his fault. I was left in pieces on the road. I should be glad that they managed to fix me back to this degree. No more singing with the band now, but I have taken up the trumpet. That's good for your lungs when you're sitting down all day.'

'I'm sorry,' Sandy says.

'Not your fault, sweetheart. My own stupidity! Unfortunately you can't turn back the clock. Anyway, we're not really here to talk about me. I want to talk about this treasure hunt.'

But Joey is still staring at Jimmy and his face is even more red now. What's wrong with him? Suddenly he more or less starts to shout.

'You're Jimmy Black! You're from Black Rock Four!'

They look at Joey, then at Jimmy. Their mouths drop open. They all know Black Rock Four, one of the most famous rock bands in the country, in the world perhaps.

'Yes,' says Jimmy, 'that's me.' He is completely calm. 'That's me, although my real name is James Grant and these days I play the trumpet.'

Jimmy looks around, but they're all too stunned to speak. Are they really sitting here drinking herbal tea with a world famous rock star? Joey keeps staring. He just can't seem to take his eyes off Jimmy.

'Anyway, let's talk about this fortune,' Jimmy continues. His voice is softer now. 'Let's talk about the events of last

Sunday afternoon. I don't suppose you have found a way to get the secret message back from your class mates?'

He shakes his head.

'They came up to us, yesterday in school,' says Isabella. 'They say they know everything about the fortune. They say they know where the fourth stone is. We think it's bluff, but they have the message and know that it's important.'

'I'm going to try to get one of them to talk,' says Sandy. 'Tony. We think he may not be able to keep it to himself for long and he doesn't know me.'

'Perhaps we don't need to.'

Jimmy looks at Steven.

'I know everything happened very fast on Sunday. When you found the capsule in the stone under Hermes' foot, did you think it had been there for a long time?'

Steven hasn't really thought about this. Why would that matter?

'I don't know,' he says. 'It came out quite easily.'

'I just wondered,' says Jimmy. 'Would it be possible that someone else could have found it before you?'

'How?' says Isabella. 'Would they have found it and put it back? Why?'

'I don't know why,' says Jimmy, 'although if I had found it by accident, without knowing its purpose, I think I would have put it back. Some things in the world are best left undisturbed until fate or destiny calls for them.'

They all look at the rock star, waiting for him to continue. Clearly he has something in mind.

'When you read out those lines to me on Sunday in the garden,' Jimmy says to Isabella, 'I was rather struck by them. I was amazed by the poetic power contained in those simple lines. The words seemed so determined, so strong, as if they were there to change the world. It's something I've always tried to achieve with my songs, to make them sound true. Somehow those four lines and the mention of the stone sounded familiar to me, although I was sure I hadn't heard them before.'

Jimmy pauses, but none of them dare interrupt him.

'Last night I worked out what those words reminded me of. I remembered I had read something with a similar feel of mystery and power. Excuse me a second, will you?'

Joey has to move his knees sideways to let Jimmy through. Jimmy goes over to a small side table near the doors of the lounge and picks up a large book. He lays it on his knees, turns his wheelchair and moves back to the tea table.

'This here is the Albaston Manor guest book,' he says. 'It makes interesting reading. You will find quite a few celebrity names in this book. I can assure you that I'm not the only rocker who comes here for support.'

Jimmy turns the pages of the book while he speaks.

'Now to the point! Many of us write messages in this book. When we leave we like to encourage others coming after us with a note of spiritual healing. In the garden yesterday, whilst you were going round those statues, I remembered that one of these messages had a similar ring to the words you have been working with. Ah, here it is.'

Jimmy's left hand stretches the page flat. He moves his right hand to point at the handwriting at the top of the page.

'This was written by Roger Brittle. You may not have heard of him. He was the Poet Laureate years ago.

Unfortunately he had to resign when his drinking got out of hand. He died later on, but according to this book, he was here at Albaston Manor in April 2006. And this is what he writes.'

Jimmy pauses briefly, before he reads:

The Wheel once Turned
To the Count of Ten
The Fourth Stone, over Hissing Heat
Is in the Dragon's Den

'The fourth stone,' Steven says quietly. He can hardly believe it.

Jimmy goes on. 'The first time I read these words I didn't get it. No idea what it meant. But as it was a poet who had written them down, I didn't mind not fully grasping their meaning. But since yesterday, when you told me your story and read me those other words, which clearly mean much to you and to your attackers, I have been thinking that these words here are the ones you are looking for. That fourth stone is a bit of give away, I would think. I wonder if, when he was staying here, Roger Brittle found that capsule under Hermes' foot by accident. He liked the words and decided to write them down for others to see. Perhaps he also chose to preserve the mystery and put the capsule back where he had found it. I would have done the same.'

Jimmy finally stops speaking. Could it be true? Could he be so lucky that the message he lost so stupidly to Andrew and Tony has - out of the blue - presented itself with hardly any effort? Jimmy could be right. The tone and style of the words in the guest book are so similar to the other two verses. The fourth stone is mentioned. These words have to be the ones they are after. It has to be as Jimmy thinks. It's almost too good to be true.

He looks at Jimmy. Suddenly he feels the blood draw away from his face. 'The B-broken Man!' He stammers. 'The Broken Man is you!'

They all look shocked. Do they not understand it?

'The Broken Man the One You Need,' he says. 'In the verse of the third stone. We thought it was one of the statues, that one of the statues would be broken. But it has nothing to do with that. The broken man is .....'

He stops speaking. Suddenly he isn't sure whether its wrong to talk about Jimmy in this way.

'Me?' Jimmy says. 'The Broken Man is me? That's strong.'

He's not cross to be called a broken man. He's surprised. They're all surprised. If Jimmy is the broken man from Thomas Carpenter's verse, it is even more likely that the words in the guest book are the ones they are looking for. Someone, this poet Roger Brittle, has found them before, put the capsule back, but made a note of the words in the guestbook. It doesn't matter any more that he lost the capsule when Andrew snatched it away. But how could Thomas Carpenter have known about Jimmy, about Jimmy being in a wheelchair?

'This is weird,' says Joey.

'Unreal,' says Sandy.

'If this is true,' says Jimmy, 'if I am the broken man, then these words are even more powerful than I thought. Powerful and mysterious.'

'Can I have a look at the writing in the guestbook?' Jimmy hands the book over to Isabella. She reads the new lines out again: The Wheel once Turned, To the Count of Ten, The Fourth Stone over Hissing Heat, Is in the Dragon's Den.

There can be no doubt about it. These are the words they need. They have to be Thomas Carpenter's words. What does it matter that they don't have the original writing? With Jimmy's help they now have exactly what they need to continue their search. He feels more certain than ever that he's meant to find the fortune.

11 Bikers

'He can't mean a real dragon's den,' says Isabella. 'Dragons don't exist.'

Steven looks out of the lounge window. Two days ago he was out there by the pond, wet and bloody, and more angry and frustrated than he had ever been. Now he sits here drinking herbal tea with a world famous rock star and is back in control. Almost. The roadsign to the fourth stone, the new verse, had been here all the time. They are getting closer. But there's no time to lose. This time they have competition. It's dead certain that Andrew and Tony are also trying to find his fortune, maybe with help from others. Isabella thinks they won't be able to work out what the message means. He's not so sure. Tony and Andrew are two days ahead of them, two days to decode the words and find the location of the fourth stone.

'What about that hissing heat?' says Joey. 'If it isn't a dragon, then it's certainly something that is very angry.'

'Poetic license,' says Jimmy.

Steven opens his mouth to speak, but closes it again. He's still thinking about Jimmy being the broken man. How could Thomas Carpenter have known? It sends a shiver down his spine. Something strange is going on, something he can't understand. What had Mr Liddell written in his letter? We are like dust in the universe and we have little control over what happens in our life. Jimmy is the broken man. He is not only broken - literally - but also a famous rock singer. The One You Need. Jimmy now seems to be the newest recruit on his team. His team!

Steven Honest, stutterer turned treasure hunter.

'It's an old mine,' says Sandy. 'Hissing heat - that sounds like steam to me. Many of the mines had steam engines. They were introduced in Thomas Carpenter's time and he was a miner himself, a Mine Captain.'

'And wheels,' says Isabella. 'Mines had waterwheels too, for hoisting things in and out of the mine shafts.' She sneezes.

'Are there many mines around here?' Jimmy asks. He's the only one who doesn't know the area well. Of course. He must be staying within the walls and security of the manor house most of the time.

'There are so many,' says Sandy. 'In Thomas Carpenter's day the place was heaving with mines. It was a big industry. You can see the remains everywhere. Old mine chimneys and falling down engine houses.'

'Thomas Carpenter was from Wheal Argon,' Steven says. 'That's where I live. Practically opposite our house there's an overgrown woodland which used to be the mine site.'

'He mentions copper and tin on his gravestone,' Isabella adds. 'Tin and Copper for the Lord.'

'There is also Wheal Zion, Wheal Lucy, Wheal Edwards, Drakewalls, Wheal Francis, Wheal Martha,' says Sandy, 'not forgetting Morwellham and the Devon Great Consols of course. The smaller mines were often started by one or two men. Sometimes there was a rumour of a seam of tin or copper somewhere and they would just start digging. If they were lucky they found a rich lode of minerals. They would then register the mine quickly, often named after the first owner or sometimes his wife.'

Steven tries to remember what Thomas Carpenter had written in his testament. Had he mentioned a steam engine at Wheal Argon?

'I have heard about Morwellham,' says Jimmy. 'What about Drakewalls?'

'That is towards Horleycombe,' says Sandy. 'I think it's named after Sir Francis Drake.'

'Drakewalls is cool,' says Joey. 'Good biking! There is a really fast track through the old mine. We call it the Den.' Before he finishes his sentence they all know that he has said something important.

'Drakewalls Den,' says Jimmy slowly. 'That is interesting. A friend of mine, a singer, is called Drake. We call him the Dragon.'

'Drake could easily be an old word for dragon,' says Sandy. 'Drake, Dragon - it is not far out. The Spanish called Frances Drake 'El Draque', which means dragon. I know that Drakewalls Mine definitely had a steam engine. It was one of the first mines to start experimenting with steam.'

Could Drakewalls Mine be the 'Dragon's Den'? It seems obvious, too obvious almost. But if it is, there's also a considerable chance that Andrew and Tony have already worked it out. If the bikers know this mine as the Den, Andrew and Tony could have easily made the connection. He knows that it's decision time.

'If this is right,' he says, 'if Drakewalls Mine is the Dragon's Den we are looking for, we must move quickly. The bikers call this mine the Den. If Tony and Andrew are serious they'll work it out for themselves. If the fourth stone is at Drakewalls we have to get there before they do.

If it's not too late already.'

'It's too late now,' says Isabella. 'I mean, it's too late today.'

She points outside where it has gone completely dark. The afternoon has passed by while they were sorting out the Thomas Carpenter Affair.

'Tomorrow after school, then?' he suggests.

On Wednesday when school finishes they are ready to set off to Drakewalls mine. Isabella says she's getting a cold, but she insists on coming along anyway. They take care that Tony and Andrew don't see them go. The two of them seem to be in a hurry themselves.

Yesterday Jimmy said that he also wanted to come to Drakewalls, if they would let him. Of course. The more eyes and brains, the better. So Jimmy is now officially a member of the team. And he's a celebrity! Only Sandy can't make it. She has to work again. But she said they should go anyway to see what they can find out.

Drakewalls Mine is a familiar spot. Steven has passed it so many times. He used to come here with his dad, when his dad wanted a Saturday paper from the newsagent nearby. Joey probably knows it even better, having practised his biking skills in the Den. Would this be the place? Weird to think that a new message might be hidden here.

This afternoon he sees the remains of Drakewalls Mine in a different light. It isn't difficult to imagine this place as the den of a real dragon. The stump of a square structure made of dark stone towers over the site, possibly a remaining support for an enormous waterwheel. On the right a tall arched gate opens to a secluded space behind. Joey explains that this part is really the bit that the bikers call the Den. It's surrounded by a ring of inward facing slopes. The earth everywhere is densely compacted, probably by years of passing shoes and bicycle tyres. The old mineshaft is on the left. It's a dark black hole that disappears into the earth, many hundreds of metres deep.

Steven hears the words of his father echo in his mind. 'Don't go too near, Steven! You're too young to be a miner.'

The mineshaft is fenced off with wire to stop people getting close to the edge, although in places the fencing has gaps. Anyone stupid enough to go through could easily risk their life. Behind the den there's another stone structure, a wall half leaning against an earth mound. Behind the wall a tall round mine chimney rises high above.

They leave their bikes in the stand at the Information Centre. There's a white van parked near the entrance gate.

'Jimmy's?' Joey wonders.

As they go through the stone arch they see that Joey was right. Jimmy is in the middle of the Den. He looks small in his wheelchair, surrounded by the massive black granite remains of what had once been Drakewalls Mine.

'Hello, my friends,' Jimmy says. 'I wish I had brought my trumpet. This place has excellent acoustics.'

Last night Steven looked up Jimmy - James Black - on the internet. Joey and Isabella said they'd done the same. The number of web pages was incredible, an overwhelming stream of evidence of Jimmy's fame. And yet, here he is today addressing them as his friends. Jimmy's first remark was about music. He's a musician through and through, living and breathing music wherever he goes.

'So where do we start?' says Joey.

'I was looking at the information plaque earlier,' says Jimmy. 'It mentions the steam engine, but I can't work out how exactly these bits of wall relate and where the steam engine would have been. As it says 'over hissing heat', I guess we should be looking somewhere above where that steam engine once was.'

'Let's hope that wherever it is, it's still here,' says Isabella.

It's not like her to be pessimistic. Her voice is croaky. She's definitely getting a cold. She has a point, of course. If Thomas Carpenter has concealed his next message somewhere on this mine site, there's a good chance that it's now lost, together with all the parts of the buildings that have disappeared. But they have to think positively. Any concealed message might have survived, just as these remains of walls and the chimney are still standing.

'We need to look for something that can be counted,' says Joey. 'I think the riddle says we need to count to ten.'

They all start scanning the walls around them, searching for ridges or turrets, features in the wall structure that could be counted. It reminds Steven of Penny Cross. He and Isabella had thought eleven giants and five dwarfs might mean a specific pattern of stones, when it turned out that the numbers meant something quite different. He suddenly breaks out into a cold sweat. Does the number this time also refer to a month or a date? October? If that's the case, he'd have to wait a whole year before it's October again, or almost a month before it's the next tenth day of the month. He can't bear to think about it. Hopefully it will be different this time. Hopefully they'll discover something here to help them find the next stone. If only he knew more about the mine. Where would the steam engine have been? How was the waterwheel constructed?

'I'm going up,' says Joey. He is close to the back wall, the one built up against the earth. There are some steps next to it. From there Joey pulls himself up and gets on top of the wall. If, as Jimmy said, the words 'over hissing heat' indicate a place somewhere higher up, it would make sense to investigate the building remains from a higher level.

They look on as Joey climbs up the slope and heaves himself on to the wall. It appears to be solid and wide and Joey can step on top of it easily.

'Good view!' he calls out.

'What can you see from there?' says Jimmy. 'Anything different?'

Joey looks out over the mine site below him. The Den is like a spider, like a star shaped creature with tentacles in five different directions, drifting out between the various remnants of buildings. The mineshaft is on his right. It's a dark hole, as if it's the creature's gaping mouth. It could be a kind of dragon. Joey pictures smoke bellowing out from the dark pit and the mine coming alive with people and movement, men dragging heavy loads from the earth, hammers clanging, a wheel turning. It would have been noisy and dirty, quite different to the mine today. Joey lets his eyes move sideways from the mineshaft to the arched gate. The colour of the stones is darker on the right hand side of the arch.

'Something there,' he calls out. 'The stones on the right are different in colour.'

They all turn around to the wall that Joey is pointing at. Steven sees what Joey means. The markings of some stones are indeed much darker. They are practically black as if they've been burned.

'Look!' Joey shouts. 'Some of the stones come forward. They look like steps.' His arm is now making wild movements through the air, pointing out a diagonal of stones sticking out. The stones that he is waving at stick out from the wall by a foot or so. Perhaps they were intended to support roof beams that had rotted away or were burned? Or perhaps they had been steps? Steven starts counting. There are only eight, but there are also two gaps in between. There would have been ten! The highest one is close to a small platform, almost at the top of the arched gate, frighteningly close to the dark hole of the shaft below.

'We have to get up there,' he says.

Easier said than done. The steps stick out just enough for Steven to stand on, but not comfortably. There is a half metre void between each step. He has practically nothing to hold on to in the wall. The only support he has is each next step. He's determined to see how far he can get and steps on to the first stone, keeping his body close to the wall. He manages to get up to the second, then the third step. This is where it's getting tricky. Where the fourth step should have been there's a gap. He can touch the next step, the fifth, with his hand, but to get his feet on to it is much more difficult. The gap he has to bridge is almost a metre wide. Fortunately he's not yet too far above ground level. If he falls he'll probably get away with bruises only. He leans his body forward and stretches out his arms. With his left hand he takes a firm hold of the fifth step. Pushing himself on to his toes he can just about reach the sixth step with his right hand. Without thinking about it any further he launches himself into the air. He closes his hands firmly around the two steps that he can touch and manages to get his knee on to the edge of the fifth step. Painful! His two hands and one knee now carry his full weight. Slowly he pulls himself up until he can stand up again, now with both his feet on the fifth step. He has to rest for a moment to regain his strength and looks down. He is now close to three metres above ground level. The only way forward is to continue climbing up. How to get down again is something to worry about later.

The next few steps are easier. Steven needs to keep his body close to the wall. The main thing is keeping his balance. The wall is quite rough here, which helps him to find support. He realises he is stuck to the wall here like a spider. He avoids looking down at Jimmy and Isabella. He can feel their eyes on him. He carefully moves up to the next step and the following two. With every one of them his distance from the ground gets bigger. Falling now would leave him with more than only bruises.

Where the ninth step would have been is another gap. Almost four metres above ground level, he isn't keen on repeating his earlier stunt. But he's so close to the top of the wall now. He stretches himself in full to hold on to the top ridge. This way he's able to step on to the last protruding stone without too much difficulty and from there on to the platform. He has about a square metre to stand on, still holding on to the top of the wall. He won't need his balancing skills for a while. But as he lets his eyes wander away from the wall a queasy feeling pierces through his stomach. Up here he is only about three metres away and perhaps five metres above the gaping hole of the shaft. He looks down into its nothingness, into its threatening black opening, keen to swallow up everything and everyone unwise enough to get too close.

'Are you OK?' Isabella calls out in her faltering voice.

'Anything there?' says Jimmy.

Steven forces himself to look away from the dark pit and concentrates instead on the wall above the arch. He moves his hands over the surface and feels the stones. They are cold under his hands. He pulls at some of them, hoping that something will move, but all the stones in the wall are firmly locked in place. A relief in one sense.

'Nothing obvious,' he bellows to his friends below. Has he climbed up here for nothing? He keeps looking along the wall and turns around to look over the mine from his high viewpoint. A stone in the platform under his feet moves. It's only the tiniest of movements, but it doesn't escape him. He places his feet apart and carefully kneels down. One small block of granite in the platform under his feet has a wider gap around it. The mortar has worn away and the block moves when he pushes it. He tries to get his fingers in the gap, but the space is too narrow. He needs something thin to lift up the block. The only thing he can think of is the buckle of his belt. He takes his belt off and pushes the buckle into the gap. Can he force the block upwards? It works. He manages to jack the stone a tiny fraction upwards, just enough to get his fingers around it. His heart beats fast when he lifts it out of its socket. The willingness of the stone to be lifted is telling. He already knows that he has found what he wanted. In the space he has opened a familiar shiny cylinder lies staring up at him.

'I've found it,' he shouts. 'It's here! I have found the capsule.'

He sticks his hand in the opening and takes out the cylinder. It's exactly like the others. It fits perfectly in his hand, as if it's telling him that it is glad to be found after so many years. But he's still at a precarious height. He has to keep his head cool. He slips the cylinder into his pocket and puts the stone block back in the opening. He also has to refit his belt through his trouser loops before he can start the climb down.

The first step down from the platform is easy, holding on to the upper edge of the wall. Then he must navigate the bigger gap, where the ninth step is missing. Perhaps if he sits down on the top step he would be able to dangle his legs down on to the one below the gap.

Suddenly there is movement in the Den below him. To his horror he sees eight boys ride their bikes through the arched gate into the mine area. They stop with screeching brakes in front of Jimmy and Isabella and jump off. Almost immediately they look up at him.

'Looks like you've done the work for us!' It's Andrew. Of course. Tony and six others bikers are with him.

'Thanks for announcing so clearly that you've found it. Another silver secret! Well done, friend! Best give it to me!'

No way! Steven is in no mind to surrender, but he's in a difficult position. They can't reach him, not easily, but neither can he go anywhere himself. He's literally stuck against the wall up here.

'Forget it!' he says. 'Why would I give it to you? It belongs to me, not you.'

'Not sure I agree with you there, mate,' says Andrew. 'You see, we already knew it was here, this fourth stone and its little secret. Us bikers, we already knew that this is the Dragon's Den. This place happens to be our territory. Ask your friend Joey. So this pretty treasure belongs to us, you see. To make things a bit easier, we thought it best to leave the detective work to you and your funny friends. After all, you're our teacher's pet. We were just waiting outside for your announcement of the good news. Now throw it down!'

The bikers grin. Andrew is their leader. They like what he says.

'I'm not giving you anything,' Steven says. 'If you want it, you'll have to come and get it.'

'I'll go,' Tony says immediately. 'I'll climb up there to take it from his little hands. Looks like he wants another bloody nose. Might just give him a little push too.'

Andrew puts a hand on Tony's arm. 'Not necessary,' he says. 'I'm sure little Steven up there will give us the capsule of his own free will.'

Andrew stares straight up at him, without saying any more. All of the bikers stare at him. He looks straight back, not saying a word, just doing his best not to look intimidated.

'Well?' says Andrew. 'Is your free will coming into action or does it need a little shove?'

'Forget it!'

Steven doesn't know what Andrew means, but he's safe here. If any of them is planning to climb up here, they'll have a hard time taking the capsule from him.

'Some encouragement then,' says Andrew. 'Shall we do the old man or the girl? Let's start with the old man.'

He gestures to the bikers. Tony and three others surround Jimmy and start pushing his wheelchair towards the mineshaft. Jimmy tries to hit out at them, but in his sitting position he is no match for the three bikers around him. The other three stay close to Isabella.

'You would never do that!'

'You'd be surprised.' Andrew voice is chilling. 'Or would you prefer it if we chuck down your girlfriend first?'

The three boys near Isabella grab her by her arms, in case she tries to run.

'Well, teacher's pet?' says Andrew. 'Time to make up your mind. Who are you getting rid of first?'

The four boys push Jimmy further towards the edge of the pit. Stones fall on the other side of the Den. Joey comes down from the opposite wall, half jumping, half sliding. He runs towards Jimmy and the four boys and tries to push one of them away. But Joey is no match for them. They easily push him aside and continue forcing Jimmy closer to the edge of the mine pit.

'Stop!' Steven puts his hand in his pocket, takes the capsule in his hand and holds it up in front of him. 'Is this what you want?'

'How did you guess?' says Andrew. 'Throw it to me.'

'No!' he says. 'If we're not to have it, neither are you.' With one swing of his arm he rockets the capsule towards the black hole of the mine.

Isabella realises what he's trying to do. If the capsule disappears into the hole and is lost, Andrew and his friends have no more reason to push Jimmy or her into the mine. Perhaps Steven has already read the message, so that they don't need the cylinder anymore.

Things turn out differently. Despite being so close and almost above the mineshaft Steven's throw is poorly aimed. The capsule lands with a dry sound on the edge of the pit. It bounces and rolls against a rock. Andrew takes a few steps and picks it up.

'Nice try, mate,' he says. 'But you missed. Lucky for your friends!'

'Lucky for your friends!' repeats Tony. He and the other three give Jimmy another push. His wheelchair tumbles over and Jimmy falls to the ground, less than a meter away from the shaft.

Isabella is luckier. The three surrounding her just let her go. The bikers have done their job. They pick up their bikes and start leaving the Den, Tony and Andrew last.

'Don't forget to give the old man his pills,' shouts Andrew as he cycles away through the arched gate. 'He may need them.'

Steven makes his way down as quickly as he can. Joey and Isabella are helping Jimmy back into his wheelchair and push him to the centre of the Den. He seems to be alright.

'I shouldn't have come,' he says. 'I'm more hindrance than help to you in my chair.'

'There were just too many of them,' Joey says. 'I know what they're like. We wouldn't have had a chance anyway.'

'Did you open it?' says Isabella. 'Did you read what it said?'

Steven doesn't answer her. He first takes a few steps towards the arched gate to see if the bikers have really left the scene. Then he faces his friends.

'No,' he says. 'I didn't have a chance to open the cylinder. I didn't see the message inside, at least, not yet.'

He holds his fist towards them and opens his hand slowly, revealing in the palm of his hand the perfect shape of the silver cylinder that he has just taken from under the fourth stone.

12 Miss Henderson

'I don't understand,' says Joey. 'You threw it down! You tried to throw it into the mine, and you missed, and Andrew got it.'

Isabella and Jimmy look at Steven. Jimmy begins to smile.

'I did throw it down,' Steven says, 'but I didn't miss. I didn't want it to land in the mine. I wanted Andrew to get it, because ... it's a fake.'

'You're a genius,' says Isabella. Joey still looks baffled.

'After the last time at Albaston, I was so cross with myself for letting Andrew snatch the message from me. We knew they kept an eye on us, we knew they were suspicious, and still I didn't expect their attack. I told myself to be better prepared next time. So I made up a fake message and put it in one of the earlier cylinders, just in case. As it happened, it worked out perfectly.'

'Nice one,' says Jimmy. 'I'm glad my life wasn't at risk needlessly.'

'I'm very sorry about what they did to you. What they threatened to do.'

'I doubt that they would really have pushed me into the mine,' says Jimmy. 'Murder is a different thing all together. But that is by the by. I'm not dead. Aren't you going to open it?' With a nod of his head Jimmy indicates the capsule in his hand.

Steven looks once more through the arched gate to make sure that they're still on their own. There isn't a sign of the bikers. He takes both parts of the cylinder, twists them and pulls both halves apart. Inside, to everyone's relief, is the rolled up fragment of paper they hope for. He unrolls it carefully and reads it. His eyes need to adjust again to the old fashioned curls of Thomas Carpenter's handwriting. The others stand silently around him. When it's clear to him what it says he reads it out to his friends.

Seasons Turn in our Father's Hand
Two Horses Fierce and Strong
A Rose over the Winter Land
The Endless Fifth Unmoved Too Long

'Cool,' says Joey.

'Poetry, once again!' says Jimmy. 'Splendid!'

Isabella wants to say something too, but she can only swallow. Her voice is really giving up now. Steven too is lost for words. He suddenly feels tired, exhausted by the cruel rhythm of this treasure hunt. Every excitement, every bit of success is instantly followed by a new challenge. No 'thank you', no 'well done', no encouragement! Every time his only reward is yet another series of words, poetic perhaps as Jimmy says, but all the more cryptic and strange for it! How can they ever work out what these new lines mean?

'We'll have to think about this one,' says Joey.

'At least we now all know this new riddle,' says Jimmy. 'We can't lose it anymore. We must try to memorise the words, as if they're a song.'

The new riddle is no easy one. They're not going to solve it here and now. It's time to go home. They leave

Drakewalls Mine - the Den - and walk back to their bikes. Not the brightest idea to leave them there, as a clear signpost. Fortunately the bikers haven't touched them. Jimmy goes over to his van. He opens the side door with the remote control on his key. From behind the door a floor panel comes out. With another control Jimmy lowers it to ground level and moves his wheelchair on to it. It's cleverly designed. Jimmy can get into the van and even into the driver's position without leaving his wheelchair. He lowers the side window. 'All hand controls,' he says, as he starts the engine by pushing a button on his dashboard. 'Pretty nifty, don't you think?'

'Give me a call when you need me,' he says. 'I will have a quiet think about our new challenge. Don't worry! We will work it out! Pure poetry!'

When Jimmy has driven off they get their bikes. The light starts to fade. Steven feels the coldness of the air around him. It's good to get cycling again, after that last half hour of standing still, negotiating and discussing the meaning of the new message. He can tell that Isabella is feeling the cold too and is eager to be home.

'Steven,' says Joey after a while, when they're cycling alongside each other. 'If the capsule you threw down at Andrew was a fake, what message did you put inside?'

'Something I made up,' he says. 'I copied Thomas Carpenter's handwriting to make it look real and I made the paper that I used look old.'

'But what message? What did you write?'

'I wanted to make it vague and difficult to understand,' he says, 'but it also had to make some kind of sense. I decided to send them to Oakendale Castle, if they can work that out at least. I was thinking about all the swords and axes I saw in the Great Hall and I used those for inspiration. So I wrote this for them: *A castle on the riverbank, the metal sharp as blades; behold the fifth stone in a secret room, where justice will be made.* They will have to buy a ticket to get in.'

'Cool.'

Steven catches Isabella's eyes. Not that long ago she had teased him about reciting her some poetry. She'll have to admit this is getting close, although not very romantic and written with a different purpose altogether. He can't help feeling pleased with himself.

'I wanted to get them off our backs. If they are clever enough to work out that I took my inspiration from Oakendale and they're going to have a nose around there, then at least Sandy can keep an eye on them.'

'It's brilliant,' Joey says, 'but risky too. You didn't know what the real message would say. It could have led in the same direction.'

'That's true, I suppose.' Steven has to admit that Joey is right. 'I suppose it still could. We have no idea yet where to look for the fifth stone ourselves. I have no idea. But I had to come up with something. It would be an incredible coincidence if our new message is sending us to the same place. I don't think it does. Do you?'

'I hope not,' says Joey. 'Right now my mind is pretty blank. We need to let it sink in, I guess.'

That evening Steven shows the fragment of paper with the four lines of his new riddle to his mum. He tells her how he managed to send Andrew and his friends off on the wrong track. She says she's worried. Telling her that the bikers threatened to push Jimmy into the mineshaft doesn't help. But his mum also has suggestions about what the new message could mean. A farm somewhere? Land, horses, seasons - it all has something to do with the work of a farmer. Bridge Farm again? Seems unlikely. So far all the four messages have been hidden in different places. He knows that the answer is right here before his eyes, hidden in the words that Thomas Carpenter has chosen to use. It definitely is like a chess game. The options for moving the different pieces are enclosed in the sixty-four black and white squares. Move them in the right order at the right time and you win the game. But there are so many options! Finding the right one is the difficult bit.

He realises how little he has thought about playing chess in the last week. Seriously. Things have happened so quickly. The Thomas Carpenter Affair has taken over his life. He hasn't given Kasparov much attention lately. It doesn't feel good. Then there's the mortgage issue, having to move house. He doesn't ask. His mum doesn't mention it now, but he knows it's on her mind and hangs over her like a dark cloud. Anyway, Kasparov doesn't seem bothered. He simply ignores him and stays cuddled up on his cushion in the wicker chair in the sitting room.

Isabella is not in school the next day. Apparently her mum has phoned to say she has to stay at home with her cold. She needs to get her voice back. The performance in the courtyard at Oakendale Castle is getting closer.

In class, whenever his eyes meet those of Tony and Andrew he makes himself look upset and grumpy and pretends he's angry about losing the fourth capsule to them. Joey does the same.

'Must learn to aim better next time, teacher's pet,' says Tony in the break, with a triumphant smile on his face. Steven just turns his back and walks away, struggling to hide his satisfaction.

Without Isabella being in school the day passes slower than ever. Miss Henderson also suffers with a cold and isn't as vibrant as she normally is. And as if the day hasn't been long enough yet she asks him to stay on at the end of the afternoon.

'How are you, Steven?' Miss Henderson asks when they're alone in the classroom. 'How long is it now since you came back from hospital? Was it about six weeks ago? Are you keeping up with things?'

'It's going fine, Miss Henderson.'

'You're doing remarkably well. I always knew you had a good head for learning. Without your stutter it seems there's no stopping you. I am really impressed with your participation in class.'

'Thank you, Miss Henderson, I enjoy being at school.'

'I understand you've been helping Joey and Isabella with the poster for their performance at the Oakendale Fair? I saw a copy of it. You did an excellent job. It's good to have good friends, isn't it?' She looks at him, rather seriously.

'Yes, Miss Henderson,' he says. He keeps it neutral. 'Isabella was always a friend and Joey is too. I took the photographs at their band rehearsal. The band is really good.'

Miss Henderson keeps looking at him, waiting for him to say more. He isn't sure what more to say. He feels rather shy suddenly. What does she want him to say?

'Steven, I must tell you ...,' she starts, 'I must tell you that I spoke to your mother on the telephone at lunchtime. She told me that you were having some trouble with Andrew and Tony. I phoned her after I had spoken to Isabella's mother, when she called to say that Isabella couldn't come to school today. She said Isabella was pushed into a pond and you were as well. Is that right?'

His first thought is that his mum shouldn't have said anything. But he realises that if Isabella's mum had already talked, his own mum couldn't have lied about it. He nods.

'So what happened exactly?'

He really isn't prepared for this questioning. He thought that Miss Henderson asked him to stay on to discuss his school work, but not this.

'It's difficult to explain,' he says. 'We were in this place, looking for something, and then suddenly Tony and Andrew appeared with another friend and they just pushed us in.'

'They pushed you in, just like that, without reason? Have they been bothering you before?'

His mind races back to the attack on the cemetery and the times before that, even before his stay in the hospital, when Tony and Andrew were trying to make a fool of him because of his stutter. It feels as if they have always been on his heels. Their tactics were getting meaner and more aggressive, and they had brought their mates along. But he has his own team now, even including a rock star. Without Isabella, Joey, Jimmy, Sandy, even without his mum and Isabella's mother, he would never have got to the fourth stone. He wanted to keep the Thomas Carpenter Affair a secret, but he was probably the worst secret keeper on the planet. Without thinking about it any further he tells Miss Henderson all that has happened before. He tells her about the visit from the police officer and why he hasn't said anything about it to her in school. He tells her about the message in the gravestone, about Mr Liddell the solicitor and the inheritance. It all spills out. She listens with full attention.

She sighs when he finishes. She must have been holding her breath.

'That's what you call an adventure,' she says. 'If I didn't know you, I would have found your story hard to believe. So you say that Jimmy is really James Black from Black Rock Four and that Tony and Andrew tried to push him into the mine yesterday? And you found the next message, and Tony and Andrew didn't get it?' He nods again.

'Can I see it?'

'I don't have it with me,' he says, 'but I can tell you what it says.'

Steven is surprised that Miss Henderson is this interested, but it's a relief that she is. She could have told him to put it all aside and concentrate on his school work. He tells her the latest verse from Drakewalls Mine: Seasons Turn in our Father's Hand - Two Horses Fierce and Strong - A Rose over the Winter Land - The Endless Fifth Unmoved Too Long.

Miss Henderson repeats the words softly. It is as if she's tasting them, trying to detect their shape, colour and sound, trying to discover their character. This time he is observing her. He's waiting to hear what she will say.

Would she be able to unlock this new puzzle?

But when Miss Henderson speaks again it isn't about Thomas Carpenter's words.

'I went to see Black Rock Four twice,' she says. 'They were my favourite band when I was younger. I still have all their CD's.'

Miss Henderson at a rock concert? He doesn't quite know what to say.

'We think it may be somewhere on a farm,' he says. 'The fifth stone, I mean.'

After school he drops by at Isabella's. She's in her pyjamas on the sofa, curled up under a duvet. She looks poorly and still sounds hoarse and raspy.

'I hope I'll be OK for the rehearsal on Saturday,' she croaks. 'It's the last rehearsal before the gig.'

'You'll be fine, even without a rehearsal,' he says. 'If you sing like you did when I took the photographs, it will be great.' He tells her about his talk with Miss Henderson, that he has told her everything about the Thomas Carpenter Affair.

'It's not much of a secret anymore, but I trust Miss Henderson. Guess what? She was a big fan of Black Rock Four, Jimmy's band.'

That evening Steven sets out his chess pieces. His mind is so full of everything that he feels almost numb with information. Only yesterday they were attacked at Drakewalls Mine. Today he has told everything to Miss Henderson. Meanwhile the new cryptic words are spinning around in his head. He has searched the internet of course, typing various words of the riddle into a search engine without results. He has to forget about it for a while, think about something different. At least this time there isn't the pressure that Andrew and Tony might get there first. That's why he should now concentrate on his chess. The next club match is tomorrow afternoon. He wants to be prepared, or in any case feel reconnected with the game. Kasparov, of course, is delighted. As soon as he hears the familiar sounds of the chess pieces tapping against the wooden board his ears prick up. He leaves his cushion and jumps on his lap, watching the pieces as Steven moves them about.

When the phone rings around nine o'clock Steven has actually managed to forget about his treasure hunt and is deeply engrossed in the game in front of him. His mum answers the phone and brings it over to him.

'Miss Henderson,' she says. 'She would like a word.'

'I'm sorry to be calling so late, Steven' says Miss Henderson. 'I've been thinking about the words you read out to me. You thought it could be a farm.'

'Yes, Miss Henderson, because of the seasons, and the land mentioned and all that.'

'Exactly,' says Miss Henderson. 'I've been thinking about the first line, where it says 'our father', what that could mean. It's a strange phrase, because we don't all have the same father, unless he means God, but I don't think it could be God. Then I thought that in one way we do all have the same father, if Thomas Carpenter meant Adam, the first man.'

He waits for her to continue.

'Steven, this may be a coincidence. You probably don't

know that I go riding most Saturday mornings? I have good friends just outside Mountedge, who let me take their horses. The horses like the exercise. Anyway, the name of their farm is Eden Farm. Eden, like in the Garden of Eden of Adam and Eve.'

Immediately his brain switches into gear. Has Miss Henderson found an explanation for the first part of the riddle? Could that be it - the way she explains it - that 'Our Father' was Adam, and that 'His Land' was something to do with this place called Eden?

'Have you noticed any special stones?' he asks. 'Any irregular forms or shapes that could be the fifth stone that we are looking for?'

He hears himself say 'we'. Is Miss Henderson now part of the team too? How fortunate that he has told her about the Thomas Carpenter Affair! He can imagine her on horseback, better than he can picture her at a rock concert.

'There are so many stones everywhere,' she says. 'I can't say I have noticed any special ones. Perhaps you should come and have a look yourself? Why don't you come on Saturday morning?'

Isabella is still ill on Friday. In school Miss Henderson winks at Steven once, just briefly, as if to confirm their plan for the next day. Otherwise she is just their usual teacher again. She doesn't show in any way that she's now aware of the situation between him and Andrew and Tony, except perhaps that she directs some more difficult questions at the two of them. In the lunch break Steven tells Joey about the new plan to investigate Eden Farm.

Joey has to go to the band rehearsal. The same goes for Isabella, if she's well enough to rehearse tomorrow. Joey thinks they should also update Sandy and Jimmy. Joey offers to phone Jimmy. Steven will tell Sandy. Maybe they can come to Eden Farm to search for the fifth stone, if it is there.

On Friday afternoon he loses his match at the chess club. It's a long time since he last lost. His opponent can hardly believe it. Steven is cross with himself. Despite his practice last night he's blundering and making mistakes. He has his reputation to keep up, but he can't seem to concentrate properly. There's little he can do about it. His mind is occupied with the plan for tomorrow, when he'll meet Miss Henderson at Eden Farm and possibly, hopefully, discover another clue.

13 Adam's Burden

Steven phones Isabella early Saturday morning. She's feeling better and is determined not to miss the crucial rehearsal. He doesn't dare begin talk about the fifth stone. He hasn't heard back from Jimmy or Joey and Sandy is on weekend duty again, so he cycles alone to Mountedge to meet Miss Henderson at Eden Farm.

Mountedge village is built on the southern slope of a ridge of hills. He knows that it's famous for its views over the valley. On a clear day you can see for miles around. He has to work his bicycle hard to climb up to the village. Fortunately he doesn't need to get right to the top. At the boundary sign for Mountedge he spots the sign left to Eden Farm that Miss Henderson has told him to look out for.

The track leading to the farm is narrow, uneven and overgrown. It can't be used much. After two hundred metres, where the track comes to an end, the views over the valley open up magnificently. Even in this grey morning light it's an astonishing panorama, looking out over the irregular pattern of fields, hedgerows and trees dotted all around. Four stone farm buildings huddle together at the top of his view. A small stream comes down on the right and dips under a stone bridge before it continues its way further down the valley. Eden Farm. It truly is a small paradise. The view of it all somehow fills him with hope.

Miss Henderson is outside one of the buildings, talking to a man whilst brushing a large brown horse. The horse raises its head when it sees Steven and makes Miss

Henderson and the man also look his way.

'Hello Steven,' she says. 'Welcome to Eden Farm! Isn't it beautiful around here?'

He nods.

'This is Phil, the lucky man who lives here all year round and enjoys these views every day.'

'Good morning, son,' says the farmer. 'I understand from your teacher that you have an interest in archaeology.'

Steven nods again. He is glad that Miss Henderson has made up a credible excuse for his visit.

'Well, you're very welcome to have a look around. I think you can probably work out why it is called Eden up here, although we are not running around naked and my name isn't Adam. Ha! We also have some interesting historical features to look at. Around the back of the stables you can find the remains of a bronze age dwelling and there are some Roman remains too. Only thing we haven't found yet is that pot of golden coins. Ha, ha! If you spot it somewhere, come and tell me!'

The farmer doesn't expect him to laugh too or say anything. He just turns around and heads towards the main house. He continues talking as he walks away. He doesn't seem to mind whether anyone is taking notice or not.

'A good man,' says Miss Henderson, when the farmer is gone. 'Likes to hear himself talk, keeps his heart in his wellies and is always very generous.'

'It's kind of him to let me look around,' Steven says. 'And thank you for not mentioning the actual reason for my visit.'

'Of course,' she says, 'although I doubt whether Phil

would have been very interested. He's only joking about that pot of gold. I don't think he cares much about treasures. What more do you want when you're allowed to live here? Isn't that so, Rowan?' She strokes the brown horse over its nose and receives a friendly nudge against her shoulder in return.

'Do you like horses, Steven?'

He shrugs his shoulders. He has always been afraid of horses and they seem to sense it.

'They are majestic creatures, aren't they? It's magical to go riding. Perhaps you should try riding some time.'

He's not sure and wants to say so, but he doesn't. There's a difference now. He's not the same Steven anymore as he has always been. There's no reason to feel frightened of horses. He no longer stutters. He is on the trail of a fortune assigned to him and he has many friends to help him.

'That would be great,' he says. 'I haven't sat on a horse before, but it must be wonderful! I would like to give it a go.'

'I think Rowan here would happily take you through the valley,' says Miss Henderson, 'but not today. I believe you have work to do.'

'Can I just look around?'

'Absolutely,' says Miss Henderson. 'Phil likes to encourage a young archaeologist. Take your time. I don't think you need fear another assault in this little paradise. I must be on my way now and allow Rowan to stretch her legs.'

She puts one foot in the stirrup and swings herself into the saddle on Rowan's back. The horse is eager to go, having waited patiently for the last quarter of an hour.

'I might not be back before you are done,' says Miss Henderson. 'I hope you find what you are looking for, Steven. I hope that this is the right place. And don't worry about Phil. He honestly doesn't mind you looking around. He likes to share his paradise. Good luck!'

She makes a clicking noise, letting Rowan know they are ready to go. The horse knows the way out through the yard and needs no further encouragement.

Steven looks on as Miss Henderson and Rowan head towards the fields. When they have disappeared out of view he suddenly feels lost, alone in the farmyard. Is this really where he might find the fifth stone? What connection could Thomas Carpenter have had with this place? Without his friends his doubts come back rapidly. All the effort he's making to understand Thomas Carpenter's riddles - would it really lead to a treasure? On the other hand, he has come a long way already. So far all the verses have come true. If the fifth stone is here, somewhere nearby, and if he could find it, the seventh stone is getting closer too. Just a small step from five to seven! If he's in the right place here at Eden Farm, where should he be looking?

He starts observing the farmyard and the buildings more carefully. The main farmhouse and the stables are made of thick walls, built from natural stone. The stable buildings have wooden doors on solid metal hinges. Most of them are open anyway. The yard itself is as chaotic as any farmyard. A stack of bricks in the far corner, a rusty wheelbarrow leaning against a wall, an old plough or something similar with a bundle of ropes hanging over it. If you forget about the views this farmyard doesn't exactly look like the 'Garden of Eden'.

He decides to inspect the bronze age remains that the farmer mentioned first of all. He should at least pretend to follow his so-called archaeological interest. The settlement is around the back of Rowan's stable block. It's not much more than a half circle made by a low line of large stones and boulders. There are a couple of hay troughs in the middle. The farmer, Phil, must still be using this ancient hut for feeding his horses. He inspects each of the stones closely. None of them speak to him. None of the stones suggest they are there for any reason other than being a bronze age semi circle.

Gradually he makes his way around the various buildings on the farmyard. If only he had a clearer idea of what he is looking for! He recites the lines of the riddle in his head: Seasons Turn in our Father's Hand, Two Horses Strong, a Rose, Winter Land, the Endless Fifth Unmoved. He's not getting any further. Miss Henderson thought that this farm could be the place because it's called Eden. There are horses here too. So far so good. But what to make of the Endless Fifth? Perhaps 'Endless' meant something in the distance, something without borders? He wishes Miss Henderson was here now to think it through with him. Or any of his friends. But Joey and Isabella are rehearsing. Sandy is at work and Jimmy is probably at Albaston Manor.

His wandering is becoming random. Without any clue he begins to lose confidence. It's pointless. He walks past all the stone-made buildings, walls and features that he sees. He goes into some of the stables, even the one with the other horse inside. Nowhere does any kind of stone grab his attention, apart from a carving above the door of Rowan's stable that shows the heads of two horses. Two horses fierce and strong. The carving must have been there quite some time. On the other hand it could just be a coincidence. He has seen carvings like that before on farm buildings. And he can't see anything that could be described as 'the Endless Fifth'. He hopes Miss Henderson will return soon, but it isn't very likely, not yet. Disappointed he picks up his bike and cycles back over the bumpy track.

Back at the main road Steven sees Jimmy's van parked along the road. Jimmy is just getting out, using his mechanical wheelchair lift.

'There you are,' he says. 'I wondered whether I might have missed you. Discovered anything at Eden Farm?'

Steven shakes his head. 'It could well be the place we are looking for,' he says. 'There is a carving of two horses on the stable wall, but that's all I could find.'

'And your teacher? Is it Miss Henderson?'

'She has gone riding. She asked the farmer if I could have a look at the farm, so it was fine for me to go around the buildings, but no luck this time.'

'Do you think I might have a look too?'

He hesitates. He has inspected Eden Farm thoroughly. Why would Jimmy be able to find anything more? On the other hand, Jimmy was still a famous rock star and it mattered what he said or thought.

'You will have to push me,' says Jimmy. 'There's no way I

can do that track on my own.'

He leans his bike against a tree and takes the handles of Jimmy's wheelchair. Now that they're going back he realises that he's glad to have the chance of another inspection of the farm. There has to be something that he has overlooked.

It really takes a lot of his effort to push the wheelchair over the track to the farm. He's trying his best to avoid the dips. All the same Jimmy has to cling on firmly to the armrests. He knows that Jimmy is pretending not to mind the bumps. Jimmy continues talking. He says he was at the rehearsal of Blue River Dreams this morning. He says he was very impressed.

Steven doesn't reply. He needs all his concentration to keep the wheelchair upright. Finally they reach the farmyard.

'This is some place,' says Jimmy. 'Look at that view!'

Almost immediately the farmer appears from the main house. 'I see you have come back with a friend,' he says. 'Are you an archaeologist too?'

'This is my Uncle James,' he says, before Jimmy can answer. 'Would it be alright if I showed him the bronze stones? I mean the stones from the bronze age?'

'Good! So you can talk,' says the farmer. 'Nice to meet you, Uncle James.'

There's sarcasm in his voice, the way he says Uncle.

'Welcome to Eden Farm, and yes, by all means have a look at the settlement if it's of interest to you.'

'Nice to meet you too, and thank you,' says Jimmy. 'It would be very interesting to see the settlement, but what we are really looking for is a stone that is round or circular.

Is there any such stone somewhere on the farm that we could have a look at? We are looking for a round stone with a message inside for Steven and we have a strong suspicion that it could be somewhere around your farm.'

What is Jimmy saying? What is he doing! How can he give away the real reason why they want to look around the farm, just like that? And why a round stone? As he asks himself the question the answer flashes through his mind. The endless fifth, of course! Anything that is round doesn't have an end or a beginning, like a ring. That has to be the answer! It has to be a round stone!

'I see,' the farmer says. He's now looking at him directly. 'So you aren't much of an archaeologist then? And your teacher, does she know what you are really here for?'

He nods.

'Well, in that case, it has to be something good. Anything that Rosie gets involved with always comes good, although I don't know why she didn't tell me directly. I will have to have a word.'

The farmer seems to be alright about it. Rosie? Was that Miss Henderson's first name?

'On the matter of the stone - we do have one very big one. And round too! But it's not here on the farm. That one is out in the field. It's in an awkward place, especially when it comes to ploughing. It's stuck half underground and is impossible to move. We know it as Adam's Burden. Would you like to see it?'

'Yes please,' he says.

Steven risks looking up at the farmer. After the shock of hearing Jimmy ask the farmer straight out for what they are looking for, his hope is reborn. Impossible to move!

They might discover something after all.

'The wheelchair will be a problem' says the farmer. 'We'll have to take the tractor. Just wait here a second.'

He walks to the tractor in one of the barns and starts the engine. The engine wakes up with a groan. The farmer backs it out of the barn right to where Steven and Jimmy are waiting and lowers the trailer platform at the back of the tractor to ground level. Steven pushes Jimmy on to it.

'We'd better tie your chair to the trailer', says the farmer to Jimmy, 'to avoid any accidents.' To Steven he says: 'You'll need to hold on yourself.'

With Jimmy's wheelchair fixed in place and Steven holding on to secure himself, the farmer climbs back on to his seat and raises the trailer platform. The tractor starts moving. The farmer steers it towards the far end of the farmyard, where earlier Miss Henderson and Rowan disappeared into the fields.

They go quite a way through the fields. A couple of times the farmer gestures to him to jump off and open a gate. The fields slope down towards the valley. Then he suddenly sees the enormous lump of stone sticking out from the earth. They head straight for it. The farmer stops the tractor in front of it, lowers the trailer platform and switches off the engine. He releases the bands that hold Jimmy's wheelchair in place, and together they push Jimmy in his chair over the bumpy grass clumps towards the stone. At the same time a figure on horseback appears at the bottom of the field. Miss Henderson and Rowan stand out clearly against the sky of winter blue. She's with them in a matter of minutes and jumps off.

'Hello again, Roseanna,' says the farmer as he takes hold of Rowan's lead. 'You have chosen the most perfect morning for a ride, leaving his young man here and his uncle to investigate my farm. Turns out he is not so much of an archaeologist after all!'

The farmer stares at Miss Henderson, waiting for what she has to say, but Miss Henderson's eyes are fixed on Jimmy.

'Uncle?' she says, hesitating.

Jimmy sticks out his hand. 'Not really,' he says. 'James Grant - just a friend!'

Miss Henderson's face is bright and coloured from the riding, but that doesn't mask her blush as she takes Jimmy's hand.

'Nice to meet you, Mr Black,' she says.

'Ah, you're a fan,' says Jimmy. 'That's nice. Call me Jimmy, by all means.'

'Thank you, Jimmy,' Miss Henderson says. She's still blushing.

'Turns out,' the farmer continues, 'that what these two are really looking for is a big round stone, supposedly with a message inside. That's why I brought them to this one here in the field. We call it Adam's Burden. Did you know that?'

'I should have thought of this stone,' Miss Henderson says, 'but no, I didn't know that's what you call it.'

'The story goes that once upon a time Adam ploughed the land here. That's why we're called Eden Farm. He took the stones from the land to build the farm, but this one here he couldn't shift and the harder he tried, the firmer it got stuck in the soil. He had to leave it in the end, as a reminder that what a man wants doesn't always line up with what God has planned. That's how the story goes and why this clump here is called Adam's Burden. Others have tried to get rid of it of course, but no one succeeded. Not with horses, not with a tractor. As you can see it still has a pulling chain attached.'

The lump of stone in front of them looks as immovable as the farmer's story suggests. It's also perfectly round, like an enormous globe or cannonball that has dug itself into the earth, leaving its top part exposed to the light of the winter sun. A rusty chain of thick metal rings is attached to it in two points. They must have tried to drag it away once. The enormous boulder is about four metres wide and sticks out more than a metre above ground. How deep in the earth it sits is hard to tell. In any case, it looks precisely like Thomas Carpenter has written - an Endless Fifth Unmoved Too Long. Steven has no doubt that this stone, Adam's Burden, is the one they are looking for. Somewhere here they should find another message.

Steven walks around the stone, eyeing its surface for irregularities. He's the only one to move, the only one who has been in this situation before, with some idea of what to look for, apart from Jimmy. But Jimmy can't move his wheelchair on his own in the field. Neither the farmer nor Miss Henderson know what he is after, so the three grown-ups just watch him.

He speaks out loud. 'If this is the fifth stone,' he says, 'if this is the endless fifth from the verse, there has to be an opening somewhere.' He climbs on top of it. The stone looks impenetrable everywhere.

'There aren't any holes in this one,' says the farmer. 'There's never any water collecting on it. Smooth as an egg, it is!'

Standing on top he is as tall as Rowan. The horse has noticed it too. It makes a curious step forward towards him. He automatically steps back, forgetting that he is on a round smooth surface. He loses his balance and has to make quick backwards steps to keep himself upright, but then his ankle gets caught in the metal chain. He can't help slipping and lands backwards in the field. Fortunately this time he doesn't hit his head. Falling over in front of the grown-ups is bad enough. He quickly pulls himself up again, hanging on to the chain. The chain gives way, suddenly and he almost falls again. Where one of the rings was cemented into the stone, the heavy rusty metal has decided to let go. Is it possible that this chain, that has resisted years, a century perhaps, of pushing and pulling, now simply surrenders to his ordinary, accidental tug?

'I don't believe it...' says the farmer.

Steven is already investigating the spot where the chain has come undone. His eye finds the sparkle in the hole. He can just about touch it with his finger. 'The message is here,' he says. 'I can see the cylinder. I need something to get it out.'

The farmer has a pocketknife. 'Try this.' He opens the knife and hands it to him. He carefully slides it in next to the cylinder. By pushing the knife sideways to make contact he succeeds in lifting the cylinder up bit by bit, until it's out far enough to take hold of it with his other hand.

'The message.'

He holds out the cylinder for the others to see. It's identical to the others. Steven is in no doubt. He knows what it will contain. Miss Henderson and the farmer stare at the object in his hand. Miss Henderson must be amazed to see the words from the old rhyme become reality. The farmer is dumb-struck that the impenetrable rock on his land has so easily given away its secret.

'Open it!' Jimmy says. 'Let's see if there is a new message inside!'

Steven hesitates. As much as he wants to, he's not sure now whether he has the right. He sticks out his hand with the capsule to the farmer.

'It isn't mine,' he says. 'It's yours. We found it on your land. You should open it.'

'No, no,' the farmer says, 'I don't think so. It's you who found it. That it's on my land is neither here nor there. You knew what you were looking for and clearly this thing here wanted to be found. By you. It's yours.'

'Thank you,' he says. He is relieved that the farmer doesn't claim the capsule. He feels safe out here in the fields with the three grown-ups waiting for him to open the cylinder and check its content. How easily have they discovered this one, compared to what happened at Drakewalls Mine and Albaston Manor. Nevertheless his hands tremble as he twists the capsule and takes both ends apart. The message is securely inside, a small fragment of paper, rolled up tightly. He stretches out the paper and reveals the writing. There's no doubt that it is in Thomas Carpenter's hand. He takes time to read the old writing carefully, before he can speak the words out loud to Miss Henderson, Jimmy and the farmer, Phil. When he's sure what it says, he reads:

Let the King Sleep
While the Storm Gathers Pace
The Sixth Stone is not the Last
Fire is a Disgrace

14　Let the King Sleep

'I know how we can get into the gardens without paying,' says Tony. 'Getting into the house is going to be more difficult.'

'We have to go when there are lots of people around,' Andrew says. 'That'll give us the best chance to slip in.'

'Do we need the others?'

'Not this time,' says Andrew. 'I think this time we'll manage between us. Once we're inside the house, we'll have a good look around. See if we can locate that secret room. It can't be too difficult. Remember, we have time. Little Steven and his friends have no idea where to go next.'

'That's what we thought last time,' says Tony. 'They still went looking at Drakewalls Mine, even before we got there. Maybe the old man had something to do with it?'

'Don't be stupid,' says Andrew. 'The old man is an alcoholic in a wheelchair. What would he know about the fortune? Anyway, we can be sure teacher's pet has no idea. He threw the capsule down before he had time to see the words. That's how scared he was. As long as we keep our mouths shut, he won't have a clue where to go looking. He certainly won't be thinking about Oakendale Castle.'

'I think something is happening at Oakendale tomorrow,' says Tony. 'They always have some kind of fair in the courtyard when the Christmas garland goes up.'

'The garland?' says Andrew. 'What do you know about garlands, sissy?'

'Nothing,' says Tony. 'I had to go once with my parents, that's all. I'm just saying there will be lots of people in the courtyard tomorrow.'

Steven is sitting with Miss Henderson, Jimmy and Phil around the big wooden table in the Eden Farm kitchen. Phil's wife Maureen is serving coffee and hot chocolate.

'This is all very exciting,' she mutters, speaking to herself more than to anyone in particular. 'A treasure found in our field! Who'd have thought it possible?'

'It's not really a treasure,' he says. 'It's just a message.'

'All the same it's very exciting,' says Maureen. 'How did you know where to look?'

'That was Miss Henderson's idea,' he says. Phil and Maureen look at Miss Henderson. In a few sentences she explains about the fortune and the seventh stone. Adam's Burden was the fifth stone. She asks Steven to say the four lines of the message that has led them to Eden Farm.

'So I thought,' she says, 'that 'Our Father' could refer to Adam. That's why I thought of Eden Farm. The horses fitted in too. Fierce and strong, just like Rowan. But I didn't know that the big stone in the field is actually called Adam's Burden.'

'Jimmy worked out that it had to be a round stone,' Steven says, 'because anything that is round is endless. The only thing we have missed is the rose.'

'I don't think so.' Jimmy looks at Miss Henderson. 'I think the rose over the winter land is your teacher. Did you not see how statuesque she appeared on horseback? And after all you're called Rosie, aren't you?'

He feels a shiver run over his back. Miss Henderson is

the rose! It isn't the first time that the century old words have predicted things.

Miss Henderson blushes again. 'That must be a coincidence' she says. 'How could a Mine Captain so long ago know that I would be riding Rowan this morning?'

'There have been other coincidences,' Steven says. 'When we went to Albaston Manor the message talked about a broken....'

He stops. It feels wrong to talk about Jimmy being a broken man. Maybe that had been a coincidence after all? Jimmy doesn't seem to think so.

'First we looked at the statues around the pond to see if one of them was damaged,' he says. 'Lots of them were. In the end it turned out to be me in my wheelchair. Coincidence or not, I happened to be part of the riddle. I was a part of this young man's adventure to find out what fortune lies ahead and proud of it too. I'm in no doubt that we will get there.'

'Agreed,' says Phil. 'No coincidence, if you ask me. I have pulled that chain at Adam's Burden many times to see if it would come off. I have even tied the horses to it. It's weird, the manner in which it gave way this morning. As if it was waiting for the right moment. As if it was waiting for Steven here to come along. Some things only happen when the time is right.'

Steven feels small, listening to the grown-ups around him debating his case so seriously. The letter from the solicitor comes to his mind. Had he not written that, insignificant and small as we are, we should trust our fate? Reading that letter seems such a long time ago.

He clears his throat.

'I'm very grateful for all your help, that you are helping me find the stones and the messages. Thank you for letting me keep this.' He looks at Phil.

'I need to think about all of this. It's true that we are getting closer. I've had a lot of luck. At the same time the messages are becoming harder to understand. 'Let the King Sleep!' How will I ever find out what that means? This one is about storm and fire. How will that help me find the sixth stone?'

Nobody answers him. They study the small scrap of paper on the table and Miss Henderson reads out the words again. Let the King Sleep - While the Storm Gathers Pace - The Sixth Stone is not the Last. Fire is a Disgrace.

'It sounds foreboding,' she says. 'Steven is right. We have little to go on. It sounds as if there's danger around the corner.'

'But it's poetic as well,' said Jimmy, 'just like the other riddles. Mysterious! And we have had warnings before. I'm sure that somehow it will make sense. We need to be in the right frame of mind. We just need a little more luck. I guess we have to go with what Phil just said. Some things are meant to happen. They do when they do. At least it says that the sixth stone is not the last. We have to sleep on it, like the King as it were. Hopefully something will come to us.'

That's how they have to leave it. But Maureen continues with her own conclusions. 'I'm sure it will all come right. How exciting, a treasure found at Eden Farm!'

Phil says he'll take Jimmy back to the main road on the

trailer platform behind the tractor. Miss Henderson steps on to the platform with him and Jimmy. Back at the road Jimmy offers Miss Henderson a lift home. She blushes again but accepts.

Steven gets on his bicycle. He waves when Jimmy and Miss Henderson drive past him. Then he's left to his own thoughts. Everything is happening so quickly! They found the fifth stone. Its message is safely in his pocket. Let the King sleep! Again, it feels like a mixed blessing. He feels happy to be another step further but at the same time exhausted about having to start all over again. Where to go this time? He honestly doesn't know. He thinks about dropping by to see Isabella and tell her the news. Or should he go home and speak to her later? Try to get things a little clearer for himself first? He decides to go home. Thinking time is what he needs.

The next morning Steven wakes up early. His conclusion yesterday was that he needed time to think, but the words of the new riddle haven't stopped him sleeping. Let the King sleep! He has slept royally himself and feels revived. He has new energy to face the next hurdle. He did text Isabella last night to let her know about Eden Farm. He promised to drop in this morning and show her the new message.

Isabella's voice is a lot better. She says the rehearsal was good. She should be fine for the gig at Oakendale Castle this afternoon.

'Just in time,' she says. She says how great it was that Jimmy had come to the rehearsal.

'Perhaps he will come to the gig,' Steven says. 'Are you

expecting many people?'

'Sandy says there's a lot of interest. She's working her socks off to get everything organised. There will be lots of craft stalls and they're presenting the Christmas garland. You are coming too, aren't you?'

'Of course,' he says. 'I'm bringing my mum.'

He shows her the scrap of paper he retrieved from the fifth stone. Isabella studies the handwriting.

'I just don't know where to begin with this one,' he says. 'The words are even less specific than before. How are we to work out a location from these words about storm and fire? It makes me think that Thomas Carpenter is playing with us.'

'Perhaps there's something in the first line,' says Isabella.

'I've been thinking that too. I thought of King Arthur, and the stories Miss Henderson told us. But there have been so many different kings. It could be any king.'

'Who was king in Thomas Carpenter's time?'

'No king,' he says, 'at least not when Thomas Carpenter wrote his testament. Queen Victoria was on the throne at that time.'

'How about a king in a storm?' says Isabella. He can tell she's not a hundred percent engaged with the riddle. Fair enough. She has other things on her mind.

'I had a look on-line last night,' he says. 'There was so much. I think it has to be something from around here, but I didn't find anything. Nothing obvious at least.'

'We just have to be patient,' says Isabella. 'We have been lucky so far.'

He knows it's time to go. Isabella has to get ready for

her gig.

'Talking about being lucky,' he says. 'You should have seen Miss Henderson blush when she met Jimmy. I told you she was a fan of Black Rock Four, didn't I? Meeting Jimmy must have been quite special for her. She went all shy. Later Jimmy even gave her a lift home.'

When Steven and his mum arrive around midday the courtyard at Oakendale Castle is already full of people. It is cold outside, but dry with at least a bit of sunshine. It looks promising for Isabella and Blue River Dreams. It seems they will have a decent audience.

Lots of people are browsing around the craft stalls. Everyone wants to find their bargains before the official presentation of the Christmas garland at two o'clock. Blue River Dreams are on at half past two. Isabella and the rest of the band are setting up and sound checking. A stage has been built in the courtyard, in front of the imposing façade of Oakendale Castle with its solid medieval tower rising above it all. It must be nerve wracking for Isabella, seeing so many people out here already.

His mum wants to go around the craft market. Steven is not too bothered. He is here mainly for Isabella and the others. He has done their poster of course. It's stuck to almost every pillar in the courtyard.

As there is nothing else to do he wanders along the craft stalls too. Then he walks up to the house. The big hall is still sealed off until two o'clock, when the garland is to be revealed. He walks to the National Trust shop and browses through the leaflets. 'With medieval origins, Oakendale Castle was extended in Tudor times', he reads.

'In 1838 the house had to be adapted quickly...

His heart misses a beat.

'The house had to be adapted quickly to provide overnight accommodation for King Henry-George on an unplanned visit, due to the bad weather at sea hindering his journey.' The King had been here, at Oakendale Castle! A King! Let the King sleep! This had to be it! It had to be the King he was looking for, the one mentioned in the riddle!

He reads on. 'A bedroom was prepared in the north tower, and has been kept as the King's room ever since Henry-George's visit.' Why didn't he find this on the internet last night? He has to go and see this room as soon as the house opens!

He looks at his watch. Ten minutes to two - almost time for the garland to be revealed and the house to open. Perhaps there's just enough time to go into the house before Isabella is due to start singing at half past two. He walks back to the courtyard. Most people have turned towards the big doors and are waiting patiently. To his horror he spots Andrew and Tony in the crowd. What are they doing here? They can't be interested in the garland. Have they come to disturb Blue River Dream's performance?

Then another thought makes him want to kick himself. The fake riddle that he wrote! He himself sent them to Oakendale Castle! Are they here to look for the fifth stone? He hopes they won't see him and keeps to the back of the crowd.

The bell in the chapel of Oakendale Castle rings twice. A man dressed in a colourful historic costume appears in the courtyard. He heads for the big doors of the Great Hall. The crowd separates to let him through. With the end of his stick the man knocks three times on the door. Then he speaks loudly.

'Open up, let us in. Christmas time is nigh.'

With that the doors open slowly. The light streams into the hall. The crowd flows in too. He has to move in with everyone around him. Then the crowd stands still and gasps. Above them, all through the Great Hall, the Christmas garland stretches from wall to wall through the vast space, an enormous ribbon of green leaves mixed with thousands of red and white flowers making a bold challenge to the bleakness of the approaching winter months. The spectacle is overwhelming. The beauty of the colours lifts everyone's heart. Steven's too. If there's a heaven above its wealth and delight must be spilling over.

Slowly he manages to move through the crowd to the other side of the Great Hall, where he knows the entrance to the rest of the house is. Two people in National Trust jackets are checking people's tickets. He hasn't thought about a ticket at all. He assumed it would be free today. He'll have to go back and buy a ticket first. He remembers that he doesn't have any money on him. He'll have to ask his mum for the ticket money.

By the time he is back outside in the courtyard and finds his mum in the crowd it is almost half past two. Blue River Dreams are about to start their performance. There's no way he can go into the house now. He couldn't miss Isabella's singing. His mum wouldn't let him anyway.

Sandy walks on to the stage towards the microphone.

She taps it twice to check it's working.

'Ladies and gentlemen, thank you all for coming to Oakendale Castle today. It gives me enormous pleasure to announce Blue River Dreams, who are providing the music this afternoon. A big hand please for Blue River Dreams.'

At the sound of the clapping the Blue River Dreams musicians appear on stage - Simon, Rebecca, Marcus and Joey, followed by Isabella. Isabella wears a dark blue dress with a wave pattern and a short golden coloured jacket on top. Her long brown hair flows over her shoulders and she has coloured her lips bright red. She looks amazing! If she is nervous, there's nothing in her appearance that gives it away. She walks to her spot centre stage, lifts the microphone from the stand, and waits for the others to start the tune. He recognises the song from the rehearsal. 'Like a Dream.' Good choice! It gives a mellow introduction to the musical passion and power that he knows will follow soon. He remembers how stunned he was that first time he heard her sing. But what he remembers can hardly be compared to what happens now. Through the sound amplification Isabella's voice appears in the courtyard like a dolphin in the blue sea or like a young horse running through a meadow - strong, without hesitation and in perfect harmony with the music. The crowd falls silent. They probably thought they had come to hear a band of school kids. None of them has expected anything like the quality of sound that streams so effortlessly from the Blue River Dreams musicians on stage.

'Skate Away' is their next song. He knows it's one of her favourite songs. She gives it everything. More people come into the courtyard, attracted by the sound of the music and Isabella's clear voice. He notices Jimmy in his wheelchair at the front, close to the players and watching them intensely. Tony and Andrew are nowhere to be seen now. At first he is relieved, but then he starts wondering where they are. Have they gone into the house to look for the fifth stone? What if, by chance, they would find the sixth stone, the one he is now looking for? No chance, he says to himself. Too much of a coincidence! But he starts to feel nervous about it. What if they are looking in the house right now, whilst he is out here doing nothing? There's no stopping his thoughts now. He has to get into the house and find the King's bedroom before they do. He looks at Isabella on stage and feels guilty for not listening properly anymore. Sandy is near the back of the stage, moving along to the music. He remembers when Isabella, Joey and he went up to Sandy's office to get the posters for today printed. A moment flashes into his mind like a photograph. The staff entrance! In his mind he sees Sandy's hand over the keypad by the door. He can't see the numbers, but he sees the pattern of her hand moving as he saw her do on that day.

The audience enthusiastically applaud 'Skate Away'. Blue River Dreams start their third song, a fast number. He has made up his mind. He makes his way out of the crowd, hoping not to draw attention, and walks around to the staff entrance. Nobody is there. All the attention is focused on the courtyard. He walks up to the keypad, closes his eyes and sees Sandy's hand move over it again: top, middle, left, bottom. He opens his eyes and presses the buttons: three, six, four, nine. It works! The door clicks and pushes open. He's in the house!

He knows he doesn't have much time. He has to be back in the courtyard before the band finish their first set. The leaflet in the shop stated that the King's bedroom is in the north tower. He must first find a way from the staff offices to the public part of the house. He goes up the big wooden stairs to the first floor. Luck is on his side. He notices a door with a sign that reads 'No Access During Visiting Hours'. He opens it and enters a narrow corridor. It bends to the left and then ends in a set of stone steps, leading to an open doorway above. He goes up and finds himself coming out at the top landing of the big staircase in the main house. All he has to do is step over a blue rope with a sign saying 'No Public Access'. This is better than he could have hoped for. From here the King's Bedroom should be close, maybe only one more level up to the tower.

Below him he hears the visitors in the Great Hall admiring the garland. From outside the music of Blue River Dreams drifts in. He goes through a doorway into another room. The room is big and gloomy. There are two windows on the left, but both have blinds over them reducing the incoming light. The walls are covered with large tapestries - scenes of woodlands and hunters in faded colours. They make the room look even gloomier. He walks through to the next space. This one is also decorated from wall to wall with tapestries. Three visitors are admiring them, a man and two women. He should pretend he is a visitor too, so he stops to look at one of the tapestries above the fireplace. The head of a boar with sharp teeth sticking out is staring straight at him. It's just its head, which makes it look frightening. The boar seems very much alive. You wouldn't want an animal like that to cross your path on a walk through the woods. A shiver runs through his spine. He shakes his shoulders to get rid of it and walks on quickly.

He is lucky again. Going out at the other side of the second room he comes to another staircase, much smaller than the main stairs. It circles upwards around a stone column in the middle. This has to be the way to the King's Bedroom. He doesn't wait. He goes up the stone steps swiftly and comes to another staircase, even narrower. There is nobody around. These steps are steeper - probably too much effort for most visitors. Not for him. He flies upwards and at the top he finds what he has been looking for - not one room but two, both much smaller than the rooms on the floor below. The first room, according to a sign on a stand by the door, is the Queen's Room. Immediately behind it is the King's Room.

Steven enters and takes in the room like a detective. Quickly and efficiently his eyes scan over the surfaces and textures, the enormous four-poster bed in the middle of the room, the wall hangings and curtains, a small desk with a chair. It's as dark and gloomy as the rooms downstairs - not exactly a pleasant place to sleep. On the other hand, it's a suitable bedroom for a King. It's a serious effort to get up here via the narrow stairs. It would be so easy for maybe one or two guards to protect the King's life while he sleeps.

His eyes are drawn to the fireplace. Fire is a Disgrace! The fireplace is carved in a black type of stone, elegantly shaped with pillar-like sides curving inwards to support a stone shelf over the fire, which has two brass candlesticks on it. Above the fireplace there's another wall hanging of a boar head, staring as viciously at him as the one downstairs. He's not scared. He's more interested in the bricks in the hearth. They are not rectangular like ordinary bricks, but triangular and put together in a particular pattern. They're black from the many fires that must have burned here over the years. One of those fires had been lit to keep the King warm on that day he had come to Oakendale Castle to spend the night here - in this room! If I wanted to hide something small, he tells himself, I would find a space under those bricks. He looks closer. One of the bricks in the middle of the hearth has a darker edge around it. Has it been burned by the fire? He needs something sharp to scrape it away. He looks around him. The candlesticks! He takes off one of the candles to see if there's a spike underneath. Yes, there is. It will do.

In the courtyard Blue River Dreams finish their first set. They receive a thunderous applause as they leave the stage for a ten minute break. Isabella sees that Jimmy is most persistent in putting his hands together. Miss Henderson next to him keeps clapping too. She sees Steven's mum, Mrs Honest, looking around, probably to find Steven in the crowd.

Back stage the others all congratulate one another with high fives. They're smiling and laughing.

'We've done it guys,' says Joey.

'Fantastic,' says Marcus, looking at her. 'How brilliant that you got over your cold in time!'

'We still have the second set to do,' Isabella says. She's

pleased too that it went so well, but she is furious at the same time. The others haven't noticed Steven slip away from the crowd, but she has. How could he do that? Her best friend! He knows how important this performance is to her! How could he just walk off?

'I need a glass of water,' she says. She goes into the old kitchen that they use as their dressing room and pours a glass of water. She asks herself again. Why did Steven leave? Where did he go?

When she turns back to rejoin the others Tony and Andrew suddenly jump in front of her. Before she knows what's happening, Tony gets hold of her right arm and twists it behind her back, whilst Andrew grabs her left arm by the wrist.

'Look, it's our sweet little Diva,' he says. 'Our Diva hoping to be a star!'

'Get off me! What do you want?'

'What we want?' says Andrew. 'Not very much! Same as usual, just a little information. We just want to know where your little friend is. Your little friend, the teacher's pet.'

'I don't know,' she says. 'I don't know where Steven is. Let me go!'

'Well, at least you know who we're talking about,' says Andrew. 'You seem to agree that he was here, and now he isn't. We saw teacher's pet in the crowd outside, but he seems to have disappeared. Where is he?'

'I don't know,' says Isabella. She is not afraid of them. 'Look for yourself. Let me go! I need to get on stage.'

Outside in the courtyard Sandy is back at the

microphone and says: 'Please welcome back on stage Blue River Dreams'. The crowd starts clapping to call them back out. Joey, Simon, Rebecca and Marcus aren't sure what to do. Isabella hasn't come back from the kitchen yet. They assume she has heard the announcement and will follow, so they walk back on stage and take their positions. Isabella doesn't appear. Marcus looks at Rebecca, not knowing whether to start their intro.

'An instrumental number,' Joey whispers. 'Let's do Moonlight Dancing.'

He counts in the rhythm for Moonlight Dancing and sets it in on his snare drum.

Isabella panics when she hears her band starting to play.

'Let me go,' she screams. 'I need to be on stage. I don't know where Steven is. I saw him leave, but I don't know where he went.'

Tony holds her arm firmly twisted behind her back.

'He wouldn't be looking for a secret room by any chance, would he?' says Andrew.

'What secret room?'

'That's exactly what we want you to tell us,' says Andrew. 'We have this suspicion you see, that little Steven may have read the last note from his miner friend before he tried to throw it into the mineshaft at Drakewalls.'

'Otherwise he wouldn't have thrown it down so easily,' says Tony.

'So where is he?' says Andrew. He's not smiling anymore.

Isabella finally realises what they are talking about. Of

course! The words that Steven had made up to set Tony and Andrew on a false trail. That's why they are here today. She hadn't thought about it anymore after Steven told her and Joey the words of the message he had made up and had thrown down to Andrew. She has been too ill since Drakewalls and too occupied with today. All she wants now is to be back on stage with her band.

'If I tell you, will you let me go?' She knows that she can tell them anything she likes, because the secret room they are looking for doesn't exist.

'Tell us where your little friend is hiding, and we'll let you go,' says Andrew. 'You must be dying to do a bit more squawking out there in the courtyard.'

She has to think fast. What does she know about Oakendale Castle? Where can she send her attackers to regain her freedom and get them out of her sight? She remembers looking at the building as she stepped on to the courtyard earlier today.

'Up in the tower,' she says. 'Steven thinks it's up in the tower.'

Tony releases his grip on her arm behind her back, but Andrew doesn't let go of her other arm yet.

'You'd better be right,' he says. 'We know what to do if you're lying.'

It takes Steven longer than he wants to scrape away around the brick with the sharp end of the candlestick, but he is convinced that he's looking in the right place. The black around this brick isn't mortar. It's earth and dirt. He's sure there must be something underneath. But the sharp end of the candlestick isn't long enough.

He can't get it far enough down. He needs something narrow to slot into the gap he has already cleared to force the brick upwards. He looks around the room and sees a plastic information sign for visitors. It looks thin enough. He doesn't have time to think about it. He takes the sign and slips one corner of it into the gap around the brick. The brick moves. He pushes harder. The plastic sign snaps in his hands. He curses to himself. He didn't mean that to happen. At least it's just a sign. No historic value. He uses one of the broken shards of hard plastic to scrape away more earth. He works around the brick in the fireplace quickly until it is free on all sides. Then he slides one of the plastic shards in and pushes again. He hopes he may be able to wedge the brick upwards. It works, but he needs another plastic lever on the other side. Slowly he wiggles the old brick upwards until he can take it out with his hand. He hardly dares look when he lifts it up. He is not disappointed. Underneath, like a baby in its cradle, sits the silver capsule. Without a doubt it contains the message that will lead him to the final stone, the seventh, and the fortune to claim as his own.

He puts the brick aside and takes the cylinder from its hiding place. He's about to open it when he hears voices on the steps. In his excitement and haste he has forgotten to listen out for other visitors. They are clearly nearby. He quickly drops the brick back into place and with the silver capsule in his hand he moves away from the fireplace. He throws himself on to the floor, lifts the drape around the King's Bed and rolls himself under it. Just in time.

'He is not here,' says Tony. 'She was lying.'

A cold chill runs through Steven's body. Tony and Andrew! This is the worst thing that could have happened. Why does it have to be them?

'Not so fast,' says Andrew. From his hiding place he can sense that Andrew is looking around the room and has spotted the shards of plastic in the fireplace. He hears him kneel down to inspect the fireplace and the earth that he has scraped out. From under the drape around the bed he can see the candlestick still lying there, next to the brick, which is back in its place.

'He might not be here now, but he has definitely been here and he knew what he was looking for.'

Andrew picks up the plastic shards and works the brick upwards, just like he did himself only minutes before. He is holding his breath. Underneath they will see the empty pocket where the cylinder was hidden.

'It looks like teacher's pet got away with the family silver,' says Andrew as he stands up again.

Maybe that will be it. Now that they know it's gone, maybe they'll leave too.

'He didn't take the candlestick,' says Tony. He bends down and picks up the candlestick and the candle lying next to it.

'Unless,' says Andrew, ignoring Tony, 'unless he didn't get away. Can you remember passing anyone coming down the steps? Can you smell a rat?'

His blood freezes. Tony doesn't know what Andrew means, but he does. Before Tony has time to answer, Andrew is on his knees again, lifts the drape around the King's bed and looks straight at him in the darkness under the bed.

'Time to wake up, little Steven,' he says. 'Time to get out of bed and tell us what you've been dreaming about.'

He knows he's trapped, completely trapped. He's been stupid again. He has been too hasty in his searching and didn't think once about a possible exit route. Any other visitor would not have expected someone to be hiding under the King's Bed, even if they had noticed the broken plastic and the candlestick. Andrew of course understood immediately why there were traces of digging in the fireplace and guessed correctly that he hadn't been able to get away.

'Are you going to get out, or do we have to drag you out?' says Andrew. 'Give me that candlestick, Tony. Let's shine a little light on our ratty friend in the dark to see what he is up to.'

He takes a cigarette lighter from his pocket to light the candle.

He's sure that Andrew has seen the empty space underneath the brick in the fireplace. Andrew must suspect that he has the cylinder. There is no way he's going to get out of here. He doesn't hesitate. In the few moments that Andrew needs to light the candle he pushes the capsule, into the furthest and darkest corner under the bed. He can collect it later, once he's out of this trap. Right now it's absolutely essential that Andrew doesn't get it. The message within must have the directions to the seventh stone. It's the key to his fortune.

Andrew lifts the drape around the bed again with his left hand, whilst holding the candle in his right.

'You have nowhere to go,' he says . 'Show us what you've found or we'll smoke you out.'

'Alright, you win,' he says. 'I'll come out if you let me.'

He starts to crawl back towards Andrew. As soon as he is within reach Andrew grabs him by his jacket and starts pulling. 'Hold the candle,' he says to Tony. He hands him the candlestick. 'And block the door.'

There is no way Steven can escape now. It feels as if he is back in the graveyard where everything started more than two months ago. On his own he is no match for them and, just like back then, Tony guards his only exit. Andrew pulls him up roughly. He is not even half standing up when he gets a blow in his stomach. He almost collapses again.

'Where's the capsule?' Andrew shouts in his face.

'I don't know,' he says. Andrew punches him again. He's gasping for breath.

'It was already gone. I don't have it.' He opens his hands to show he doesn't have anything.

'No time for stories,' said Andrew. 'Why creep under the bed if you have nothing to hide.'

'I thought you were from the National Trust,' he says. 'I shouldn't be up here without a ticket.'

He takes the next blow to his stomach.

'You're lying,' says Andrew. 'You've hidden it.'

'I don't have it!' he shouts. 'I told you! It was gone already. There was nothing under that brick. Search my pockets if you like.'

Andrew is not letting go. 'Hold him,' he orders Tony.

Tony puts the candle on the floor, grabs his arm and twists it behind his back. Andrew starts feeling in the pockets of his jacket.

Suddenly flames spring up from the King's Bed. Tony

has stupidly placed the candlestick on the floor close to the four-poster bed. The embroidered textiles have immediately sucked up the flames. Before they know it the flames spread to the bed covers and start to reach higher. They all stand frozen on the spot. Tony is still holding Steven's arm and Andrew's hands are in his jacket. Then they let go. They look around the room for something to stop the flames. There's no time. The King's bedroom is full of wooden furniture and textile hangings, curtains, drapes, and covers. Everything is dryer than dry. In seconds the room fills with smoke, whilst the flames grow in size and fury.

Andrew looks at him furiously and slaps him hard in his face. He falls back on the floor.

'I'm out of here,' Andrew says. Then he just walks out. Tony runs after him. He sees them disappear through the doorway past the Queen's room and jump down the stairs. He's alone with the flames. He scrambles up, ignoring the pain in his head and stomach. He drags himself outside to the Queen's room and grabs the information stand that he has seen. He takes it back in and starts hitting the flames with the stand. He must stop the fire. He must stop it spreading! There is no point. By now the whole of the King's bed is engulfed in flames. His movements with the stand only encourage the fire. The flames reach out fast to other parts of the room. There is so much smoke that he can hardly see a thing. The capsule! He has to get to the capsule! Desperately he throws himself on to the floor. He has to find the capsule under the bed where he has pushed it away. He can't breath. It's hopeless. He starts to cough. The smoke is filling his lungs. The heat is suffocating him.

He'll never be able to reach that far under the burning bed. He must call for help before the whole room burns down. He gets himself up from the floor and with his elbow in front of his face struggles for the doorway, away from the flames. He now flies down the steps, faster even than Andrew and Tony, and starts calling out. 'F-Fire, F-Fire! There is a f-fire in the King's Room!'

15 Kasparov

Relieved to be free, Isabella makes her way back to the stage as quickly as she can. Her arms hurt. She has to ignore it. She hears the sound of the others who have started playing. She steps on to the back of the stage just as Blue River Dreams finish their extended version of Moonlight Dancing. Jimmy has somehow appeared on stage in his wheelchair and has added a superb trumpet solo to the piece. In their rehearsal yesterday he told them that it's actually one of his own compositions. He wrote it more than thirty years ago and he still knows it backwards.

Sandy is at the back of the stage. Isabella wants to tell her about Tony and Andrew, that they are roaming through the house and that somebody should keep an eye on them, but there's no time. As soon as Jimmy sees her he graciously hands over to her.

'Ladies and gentlemen,' he says into the microphone, 'please welcome back on stage Miss Isabella Carter.'

She is instantly back where she belongs. She takes the microphone from Jimmy and repays the compliment. 'A big hand please for Mr. James Black.'

The audience clap for Jimmy, first with hesitation but then thunderous. Only now, hearing his name, they realise that the guy in the wheelchair who just played that amazing trumpet solo is no one other than James Black from Black Rock Four. How could that be true, a famous rock star playing with a band of local children?

Before the break Blue River Dreams surprised with a performance more thrilling than anyone expected. Now there's no stopping them. She goes full pelt. The horrible encounter with Tony and Andrew in the kitchen has sharpened her mind. She gives it her all. She takes the audience with her in a whirlwind of musical passion, one song after the other. The people in the courtyard hardly believe what they are witnessing. She winks at Jimmy to hint that more of his trumpet solos would go down well. Jimmy is pleased to play again, raising the enthusiasm of the crowd even higher. Back stage Sandy is over the moon. She has never thought the event would work out so well, with a rock star thrown in for free.

But some way into the second set something changes in the audience. Some people start looking up rather than look at the band. Somebody has noticed smoke rising up from the tower. Suddenly there is a loud bang. One of the top windows in the tower is blasted away and flames are leaping out.

'Fire!' somebody shouts. 'The tower is on fire!'

Everyone looks up now. People are screaming, not knowing what to do. The courtyard instantly turns into chaos. People start moving in different directions. Some are standing still and looking up, others go towards the house or away from it. Blue River Dreams can't see the tower from under the stage canopy, but it's clear that something is very wrong. They stop playing.

Back stage Sandy keeps her head cool. She's already on her phone making the emergency call to 999 and instructing her team to activate the major incident plan. There is no immediate danger to people in the courtyard crowd, but there may still be people in the house. National Trust staff guide visitors as calmly as possible to safer ground. What happens up there in the tower is another matter! The bursar and a couple of groundsmen have gone up with fire extinguishers, but it may already be too late. Judging from the flames pouring out from the top it doesn't look good.

Steven comes down from the narrow stone staircase, taking three or more steps at once. His shouting has attracted the attention of other visitors in the house. There are the three people he saw earlier in the room with the tapestries. They don't recognise him. His face and clothes are covered in black. He points his arm upwards and wants to shout again that there's a fire, but no more words come. His appearance makes clear enough what he's trying to say. The man loses no time and starts tapping a number on his mobile. One of the women disappears back into the house in search of a member of staff. The other tries to calm him down. 'It's alright,' she says. 'It's alright, we are getting help.'

But it's not alright! Not at all! They haven't seen the flames! Other people come rushing up. Three men carrying fire extinguishers. They run up the stone staircase one after the other, but they're not even halfway up when there is a second bang. Another window is blown out. Accelerated by the air pulled in through the shattered windows the fire progresses to the Queen's Room. There is nothing the three men can do without risking their lives. The heat of the fire pushes them back. The narrow steps make it impossible to get closer.

It seems ages before the sirens of the fire engines can be heard. He's in the courtyard when they arrive. It must be more than half an hour ago since the candle flame had shot up in the drapes around the King's Bed. But now the hoses are connected and big spouts of water from all sides are directed at the flames at the top of the tower, where the King's and Queen's Rooms are. Were! Where the King's and Queen's Rooms had been! At first the water sprays seem to make little impact, but gradually the firefighters manage to bring the flames under control. They stop the fire spreading downwards through the tower and the rest of Oakendale Castle. The strong walls of the tower hold together, but for the two royal rooms at the top it is too late. By now the flames will have ripped mercilessly through the interior, ravaging the precious furniture and wall hangings, and leaving only stinking black rags and cinders.

The visitors at Oakendale Castle are evacuated as the firefighters take over the site. A paramedic takes Steven to an ambulance. He has to answer questions. He knows that the paramedic is checking that he's not in shock. He's fine, he knows he is, apart from the smoke he has inhaled and the black on his face, hands and clothes, and he says so.

'I'm fe-fe-fe-fine. There is nu-nu-nothing wrong with ....' He stops. His stutter is back.

'Follow my finger with your eyes,' the paramedic says. He moves his hand from left to right and back before his face. Steven does as he is told. He follows the finger with his eyes and just nods. The paramedic nevertheless insists that he must be fully checked over. He has to get into the ambulance. They'll take him to the hospital in Plymouth.

Before the doors of the ambulance close a police officer has a short conversation with the paramedic. He can't hear what they say.

'Still OK?' the paramedic wants to know again when the ambulance is underway. Again he nods. He's too exhausted to protest. His stomach hurts from Andrew's punches. He doesn't feel OK. It's hard to say what's worse – the catastrophic fire in the tower or his stutter suddenly reappearing. Not forgetting the fact that the capsule he needs for finding his fortune is still in the King's Room, somewhere in the burned out devastation up there.

At the hospital the paramedic takes him to the Emergency Department. He isn't put on a stretcher or in a wheelchair, but is allowed to walk. A specialist examines him. More questions. He gives short answers, trying to avoid stuttering, but he can't. It's definitely there.

'You have a stutter?' the specialist asks bluntly. 'Have you always stuttered or has it come on today?'

He doesn't know how to answer. Not anymore. Perhaps he really is in a state of shock? Just look in the notes, he wants to say. In half an hour I'll be fine. He doesn't speak. Regardless, the specialist declares he can find nothing seriously wrong with him.

But he isn't allowed to go home yet. He is taken to a small side room and told to wait. They tell him his mum has been called and is on her way to pick him up.

But when the door of the room where he is waiting opens, it's not his mum but a police officer. Steven recognizes him straight away. It's the officer who came to Greystone House about two months ago, when his mum insisted on reporting Andrew's and Tony's attack in the graveyard. The police officer doesn't recognise him until he says his name. No stutter this time.

'Steven Honest, you say? That rings a bell. Didn't I come and see you sometime before?'

The police officer questions him a lot more thoroughly than he did that first time. He is made to recall every detail of what happened in the tower, who had been there, how the fire had started. The officer is not easily satisfied. He is after more than just an explanation.

'I won't beat about the bush,' he says. 'This fire at Oakendale has destroyed a substantial part of the National Trust's historic collection. It's not yet clear to me what your role in all this is, but criminal charges are likely to be made.

He tells the officer everything exactly as he remembers it. He doesn't care anymore. He plainly tells the police officer why he had been there himself, how Tony and Andrew threatened him until Tony's stupid move with the candlestick set the King's Bed on fire. Sometimes he speaks fast, sometimes the stutter is back. It's not as bad as before, not like before his operation. Does it matter anyway? What more does he have to lose? He knows that the capsule with his message under the bed can't have survived the blaze. Besides, this police officer already believes that he's living in a fantasy world. Let him make up his own mind. Who cares if they think he's a stuttering idiot?

When the police officer finally stops questioning him he's exhausted. He's been seriously grilled and the officer points out again that he should expect further criminal procedures.

'I'm not sure if you're telling me the whole truth,' he says. 'We'll interview you again after we've spoken to the two others. Make sure to be at home when we need you next.'

Is he to blame for what happened in the tower? Is he to blame for the damage at Oakendale Castle? He didn't light the candle and set fire to the rooms. He tried all he could to stop the fire before it got too big. He had only gone up to the tower to look around in the King's Room. On the other hand, he had entered the house without a ticket through the staff entrance. If he hadn't gone into the house at that time the rooms wouldn't have burned down. He should have stayed in the courtyard, listening to Isabella. OK, he hadn't planned for all this to happen but in his heart he knows that he has played a significant part in the devastation.

Not guilty, but not innocent! With this stuck in his mind he faces more difficult conversations. His mum is first. He's never seen her so angry.

'How could you do this, Steven? Don't you know I have enough to worry about! Why were you up there? Why weren't you listening to Isabella like you should have been?'

It doesn't help much when he tells her. When she notices his occasional stutter she backs off a bit. She is relieved that he isn't seriously hurt and allowed to go home. At least he can tell her that it wasn't his fault. He doesn't tell her what the police officer said, that he should expect charges.

His mum insists that he phones Sandy as soon as they are back at Greystone House. He knows there's no way out of it.

'Are you OK, Steven?'

To his relief Sandy is not furious. She is calm. She has already been briefed by the police about what had happened in the tower, based on his summary of events. The police are now questioning Tony and Andrew and she will get a report later on what they have to say. The damage to the Oakendale Castle collection is clearly upsetting, but she is practical about it.

'I will have to find a new antique four-poster bed for the King,' she says. 'It can be done. After all he only slept in it once.' She doesn't mention that he used the staff entrance to get into the house. Perhaps she didnt mind that detail? After all, she had been part of the team herself.

'Whatever is going to stop you on your fortune hunt?' she asks. He doesn't answer. Without the capsule from the King's Room his treasure hunt is over. If only he hadn't left it under the bed! He tries to be calm. He tells himself that in the scale of things the loss of his fantasy fortune is nothing compared to the damage Sandy has to deal with. But he can't resist asking her if anything has been found in the King's room.

'We haven't been in there yet,' she says. 'The fire brigade has only just given the all-clear. The first inspection of the two rooms will be tomorrow afternoon. I don't hold much hope.'

His most difficult conversation is with Isabella. She is furious. No wonder. Of course she's angry about him walking away. Did he think she wouldn't notice? Couldn't he have waited? And then ruining her gig. When the fire caused the abrupt ending of their performance she didn't know he was involved. Now that she knows she's all the more angry. She was happy to be a part of his treasure hunt, but why did it have to completely ruin their success with the band?

His treasure hunt.

He tries to explain.

'I saw Tony and A-Andrew in the crowd,' he says. 'Then they disappeared. I knew they were on to s-something. I had f-found out about the King's Room. I knew the sixth stone would be there. I had to act. I had to b-be there before they did.'

He knows he isn't telling the whole truth. It wasn't just about acting quickly. It was just as much his impatience to find the sixth stone, after he had accidentally found out where it could be. Does she notice that his stutter is back?

Then Isabella surprises him.

'I wouldn't have sent them in your direction if I had known that you were in the tower,' she says. 'I just wanted them to let me go.'

'What do you mean?'

Now she tells him what happened in the interval of her performance. How she too had had to deal with Tony and Andrew, when she was needed back on stage.

'I'm sorry, Isabella,' he says. 'I shouldn't have g-gone into the house when you were playing. If only I could turn b-back the clock, but I can't.'

He can't bring himself to say that he found the cylinder, and lost it again. If he did, she would think he still only cared about his fortune, that he didn't care about having ruined her performance. His treasure, she said. She's doesn't want to be part of the treasure team anymore. What treasure? The case is over!

Isabella doesn't ask further. 'What has happened has happened,' she says. 'As you say, we can't turn back the clock.'

It's clear that she wants to end their conversation.

He stands at the top of a staircase. Behind him a corridor of red and orange flames. Miss Henderson calls him. 'Come Steven, come. Don't be afraid. Let the King sleep.' But he looks back at the flames. 'I can't,' he says. 'Tony and Andrew are in the King's Room. I have to get them out. The building will collapse.' He runs into the burning corridor. He comes to the King's Room. The walls are burning. Tony and Andrew are nowhere to be seen, but in the middle of the room there's an old man at a desk. The man looks up at him and stretches out his arm, inviting him to come in further. But the flames are all around him. Between the flames there are boars coming at him from all angles, their dripping tongues hanging between their bloodthirsty teeth. They close in on him. He must run, but he can't breathe, he can't walk, there is nowhere to go. Then there is a noise, like the sound of lightening striking.

He is awake. He is sweating all over his body. He sits up in his bed and waits for reality to replace his dream vision.

It isn't the first time that this nightmare has appeared in his sleep. In the weeks that follow the fire at Oakendale he wakes up almost every night with the visions of boars and flames raging through his brain. Miss Henderson often appears in his dream. Sometimes Jimmy is there too, laughing loudly at him from his wheelchair. Phil and Maureen from Eden Farm appear once. The old man bent over a desk in the King's room is always there. Sometimes he looks up, but he can never see his face. Is it Mr. Liddell? Is it the King?

Being back in school is horrible. The Monday after the fire Miss Henderson starts her lesson asking who has been at the Oakendale Castle event on Saturday. Many of them have.

'I'm sure you all know,' she continues, 'that the fire in the tower destroyed two of the rooms in the house as well as the precious historical objects that were kept there.'

She looks at Steven as she speaks. Andrew and Tony aren't here. He hopes she won't mention him. He feels exposed and vulnerable. How quickly things change! Miss Henderson had been on his team too, helping him search for the stone at Eden Farm. Now there's a sea of distance between them. She is just his teacher and he's just one of her pupils in the classroom.

Miss Henderson doesn't mention his involvement, nor Tony's or Andrew's. Instead Miss Henderson talks about the importance of history and the duty we all have to make sure that things of historical value are looked after.

'History is important,' she says, 'but so is the present. We'd be wrong if we were to remember last Sunday only for the fire. I would like to congratulate Isabella, Joey, Marcus, Rebecca and Simon for their absolutely outstanding performance. If anyone hadn't heard about Blue River Dreams before, they certainly won't be able to ignore them now. I have to say that I am truly proud to have such amazing stars in my class.'

It's nice that she says that.

On Wednesday Andrew and Tony are back in school. They don't try to get close to him or provoke him. They leave him alone. By now everybody knows the three of them had something to do with the fire. There is gossip that Tony and Andrew have to do some kind of community service. He knows it's true. He has to do the same. Yesterday afternoon he was called in to the police station with his mum. The officer set out the case. Apparently Tony and Andrew first of all denied that they had anything to do with the fire and said they were somewhere else on Sunday. But too many people had seen them in the courtyard. When the police confronted them with his statement of what happened and with Isabella's account of what happened downstairs, their nervous response made it clear they weren't speaking the truth. There was no evidence however that they had started the fire. They blamed him. Of course they did. Once again it was their word against his! But from the look on the police officer's face Steven knew that this time his version of events was not dismissed so quickly.

'Once again we have two contrasting stories,' the police

officer had said. 'We know that someone here is not telling the whole truth. I don't have a crystal ball. I can't see what happened up there. The good news for all three of you is that the National Trust is not pressing any criminal charges. They accept that the whole affair may have been accidental. However, beyond doubt is that all three of you were in the tower when the fire started. In light of the serious damage caused we have to set an example. Therefore I'm instructing you to make something good of the damage you have done. You are going to help with weekend work in the gardens at Oakendale for six weeks. This is not a court decision, this is my decision. If I were you I wouldn't object. It's your chance to show you're sorry about what happened.'

The worst thing about the schooldays since Oakendale is what it has done to his friendship with Isabella. Yes, he did phone her the day after the fire, and yes, he did apologise. It's clear that Isabella isn't letting it wash away. They don't walk to or from school together anymore. In the lunch breaks, Isabella doesn't seek out his company. In class she avoids working with him if she can. He doesn't know what to do. He asks Joey, but Joey just says that Isabella is still upset. 'She'll be cool in time,' he says.

He doesn't feel reassured. He feels rotten. Since his operation, when the whole Thomas Carpenter business started, Isabella had become his best friend. They had been through so much together in the last two months. He doesn't want their friendship to end like this. What can he do? He knows he made the wrong call during the gig and should have stayed in the courtyard to hear her sing with the band. But he can't change the past, can he?

In the weekends he's now working in the gardens at Oakendale. On the first Saturday Tony and Andrew were there as well. Sandy made sure that they didn't have to work together but were made to work in different parts of the gardens. Andrew and Tony didn't even bother showing up after the first day. The police officer had said it wasn't a court order. He couldn't make them. But Steven is there. At least it's something positive he can do. And he doesn't have to speak.

The other matter is of course still lingering in his mind. One evening in the first week after the fire Sandy phoned and confirmed that everything inside the King's and Queen's Rooms had really been completely destroyed. Nothing of value could be saved and nothing had been found. It was clear what she was saying. If he still had one small glimmer of hope that the capsule might have somehow, in a corner of the room, escaped the flames, Sandy's sober message has taken it away.

Without hope and without Isabella's friendship, he tries to get back into his chess. It's hard to concentrate on the games or even care about them. He tries to rekindle his fascination with the battle between white and black, but the game has lost its meaning. He just sits there, pretending. Kasparov is pleased of course. But at night he stays away. His cat doesn't like sharing the nightmares.

Steven's mum seems to understand that he needs time before he can get the fire at Oakendale Castle out of his mind. She knows he's feeling guilty for making the wrong choices. She probably guesses he's frustrated for losing the last cylinder when he was so close to finding Thomas Carpenter's fortune. She tells him that the nightmares will stop sooner or later.

She has her own worries, he knows that. She doesn't mention the mortgage issue, but there are letters. She quickly puts them away when he comes in. She's concerned about his stutter too. It hasn't been so bad lately, but she wants to get it checked. She makes a new appointment with Dr Price. He doesn't want to go, but she insists. 'We just need to have you checked over,' she says.

His mum is also sad about his split up with Isabella. Steven knows she is. He can see himself through her eyes. His stutter is back, OK, perhaps not as bad as before, but he's retreating, back into himself and into his chess games. In the last two months he had changed, he had made friends. Now he's sitting here on his own again, pretending to play chess and hardly speaking.

On Sunday morning three weeks after the fire his mum cooks him breakfast. Steven is late getting out of bed. He has to get to Oakendale but the breakfast smells great. He has half an hour before he needs to leave.

'Another bad dream tonight?' she enquires.

He nods.

'I've had an idea,' she says. 'We're going to have a party.'

'A party? Why?'

'Because something needs to change. We need to get rid of your nightmares. You have been through a rough time. I know you're upset to have lost the inheritance, to never know what the fortune was, but that's how it is. It would be worse if you also lost your friends. You need to let go.'

'I'm not sure, mum,' he says. 'Isabella won't come.'

'I think she will,' says his mum. 'There's something else too. I have spoken to an estate agent. After Christmas I'm putting the house on the market. I don't want to, but I have to. We'll have to find somewhere cheaper to live.'

There it is then. More misery coming his way. Bring it on!

'But I'm not leaving here in a cloud of doom,' his mum says. 'If I'm going at all, I'm going on a high. That's what your father would have wanted.'

'But who's going to.....'

She doesn't let him finish.

'I have spoken to Isabella's mum. She thinks Isabella can be persuaded. In fact, we have sorted out the date. It will be an Italian themed pre Christmas party here at Greystone House. It's about time that this house livens up, even if it's just for one more time. Who else should we invite? I think you should ask everyone who has helped you to search for the treasure. Although you haven't found the seventh stone, you should still say thank you to them all.'

Steven hesitates. He doesn't want to agree, but she has a point. He doesn't want to move, but if they have to leave...

She's right. He should let go of the Thomas Carpenter Affair, although that is easier said than done. He should say thank you to everyone who helped him. It's the prospect of making up with Isabella that worries him most. He is nervous about it. If she would at least come, he could perhaps start moving on again.

On the twenty second of December their house slowly

fills with the beautiful Italian smells that he recognises from his visits to Isabella. The two mothers are getting on in the kitchen. His mum seems delighted to be taking Italian cooking instructions from Isabella's mum.

Jimmy's van is the first to arrive on the drive.

'That track is almost as bumpy as the one to Eden Farm,' he says. He lowers himself to ground level on his wheelchair lift. 'I have taken the liberty of bringing my new girlfriend. I think you know her already!'

'Hello Steven,' says Miss Henderson. 'Thank you for inviting us! What a good idea to have a party, after all that has happened!'

Joey and Isabella arrive together. 'Thanks for c-coming,' he says. He feels sheepish. His and Isabella's eyes meet briefly.

'Never miss out on a good pizza,' says Joey.

They all gather together in the sitting room: Isabella, Joey, Mrs Carter, Steven's mum, Sandy, Phil and Maureen, Jimmy and Miss Henderson. They all have plates with Isabella's mum's delicious pizzas on their knees. Kasparov joins the crowd and steps around everyone's legs, hoping to have his share of bits of pizza with salami. When the eating is done he jumps on the sofa and settles in Steven's lap.

'It was mum's idea to have this party,' Steven says.

'An excellent idea,' says Jimmy. 'It's been a while since I had such a good pizza.'

'The pizzas are Giulia's work,' says Steven's mother. 'I wouldn't know where to start.'

'I'm only sorry they're not stone baked,' says Isabella's mum. 'Proper Italian pizza should be baked nella forno pietra.'

Steven knows he has to say something now. His mum had said he should. This moment is as good as any.

'Talking about stones,' he starts, 'I have something to say to you all. I want to thank you all for helping me to search for my fortune. I'm sorry that we didn't make it, that the last message got lost in the fire. I wish that had never happened.'

He didn't stutter.

'You can't unring a bell,' says Jimmy. 'Things happen.'

'Anyway, I just wanted to say thank you.' Again, no stutter. 'At least we found six of the seven stones and you've all helped me follow the trail. We still don't know if there really is a fortune and now we'll never know. That's pretty frustrating and I know I have myself to blame. But you all believed in it, you all believed in me.' His stutter seems to have gone.

'Well said, Steven,' says Miss Henderson. 'The Thomas Carpenter Affair was too exciting not to believe in.'

'Precisely,' says Maureen. 'A treasure found on our land! I still can't believe it.'

'Good things have happened too,' says Miss Henderson.

'Yes, how about me meeting Rosie?' says Jimmy. 'That wouldn't have happened without you.' Miss Henderson blushes.

'Joey and I have some pretty good news too,' says Isabella. 'Blue River Dreams have been booked for another performance. Jimmy asked if we'll play at the New Black Bean Festival on New Year's Eve.'

'That's fantastic news! his mum says. 'And well deserved

too! You were just so good at Oakendale!'

Oakendale is the word he was trying to avoid, but this time it doesn't linger.

'I can't top that,' says Sandy, 'but if we are doing good news, I have some to report as well. I just learned yesterday that Oakendale Castle has been awarded a large grant for renovating the building. We have been trying to get the funding for a long time. The fire in the tower wasn't good, but now it has worked in our favour and has helped to get us the grant.'

'Wonderful,' says Phil. 'That is excellent! It's a beautiful house and now all will be restored!'

'Anyway,' Steven says, trying to get back the attention, 'I want to say thank you for being on my side, Isabella from the beginning.'

It's definitely not happening now, his stutter. Nobody seems to notice.

'Without her I wouldn't even have found the solicitor and learned about the inheritance. You've all been great and I'm just pleased you are here tonight.'

He is stroking Kasparov as he speaks, but Kasparov decides he has had enough and jumps from his lap on to the floor. He calmly walks to the middle of the room and starts clawing the hearthrug in front of the fire. His mum tells him off and pushes him away, but Kasparov isn't having it. He comes back straight away and starts clawing the rug again, more vigorously even. With his claws he pulls up the edge of the rug and reveals a section of the slate underneath, in which Steven's father carved his son's name thirteen years ago.

'What's that?' says Sandy. 'It looks as if something is

written there.'

'Oh yes,' his mum says. She pulls back the rug further. 'It's Steven's name. When Steven was born, my husband was so proud that he wanted to carve his name somewhere. My husband was an artist. Look, he also carved the name of this house in the lintel over the fireplace.'

But all of them are still studying Steven's name, carved in the slate under the rug. He feels embarrassed. This isn't how he wanted his speech to end.

Jimmy looks at the carving upside down.

'You know, for a moment I thought it said seven instead of Steven.'

'I love to play word games like that,' says Maureen. 'Those games when you mix up the letters and make new words.' She laughs. The others continue staring at the letters of his name, as if in a trance. He looks away, embarrassed still.

Then Isabella breaks the trance. She shouts: 'Look! It says Seventh Stone! It has the same letters as Steven's name. Only the 't' is in the wrong place and 'stone' is backwards.'

She writes the letters with her finger on the slate above the letters of his name, carved by his father. The new letters that Isabella writes are invisible, but they all read the movement of her hand, and they see that she's right - that in his name there is the seventh stone.

S T E V E N   H O N E S T
S   E V E N T H   S T O N E

16 The Last Note

He is too perplexed to speak. His name is an anagram of the seventh stone?

'Magic,' say Jimmy. 'This is definitely no coincidence.'

Surely it has to be! Thomas Carpenter could never have known his name. It's impossible! By accident the inheritance has come to him. The fact that his name contains the letters of 'seventh stone' can only be pure chance. This piece of slate here in his own house has nothing to do with it. It was his father who carved out his name, not Thomas Carpenter. But his mind takes him back to Mr Liddell's office in Thornbridge, three months ago. He hears the solicitor reading out the testament. 'This is the true and lawful testament of the undersigned, Thomas Carpenter, of Wheal Argon, Cornwall.....' Thomas Carpenter lived and worked at Wheal Argon, right here. Did he once live in Greystone House?

Steven looks around helplessly. He doesn't know what to do. His mother does. 'We have to lift it up and see what is underneath,' she says. 'If anything, it may stop the floorboards creaking.'

The hearthstone is a big piece of slate. It's not at all easy to lift. Phil knows how to handle it. He takes the iron poker from the fireplace, pushes it under a corner and manages to wedge up the slate. With his and Joey's help they lift it out of its place and rest it against the wall near the fire.

Underneath where the slab was lying there's a section of old timber floorboards. On one side it has an attachment, a big iron ring lying flat in a carved out space in the timber. There is no doubt that it's the handle of a removable panel in the floor.

'Let's have a closer look at this,' says Phil. He picks up the iron ring and pulls. The panel hinges open, causing clouds of dust around the edges. Below it there's an opening, half a metre wide. The light from the sitting room streams in as far as it can reach and shows the top steps of a wooden ladder.

'Perhaps, Steven, you spoke to soon when you said we didn't find the seventh stone,' says Jimmy. 'If this isn't something to do with your fortune, I don't know what is!'

His heart beats faster than it ever has.

'We need a torch,' says Phil. 'Whatever basement is below here, it has to be significant. Someone needs to go down, at least if the ladder isn't rotten through.'

'I'll get my torch.' He runs upstairs to his room and is back within seconds. He offers the torch to Phil who seems to have taken the lead.

'I'm not going down there,' says Phil. 'It is your fortune! You must go! Besides, I think that opening might be rather narrow for me.'

They all think that Steven should go.

'We're in this together,' he says. 'At least Isabella and Joey must come down with me.'

Joey takes the torch and lights up the ladder. Steven tries the top steps. The ladder is fine and not even that tall. After eight steps he is down on the floor of the room below. Isabella follows. When she is halfway Joey hands the torch to her and she passes it down to him. Then

Joey follows Isabella and all three of them stand in the basement. Above them in the sitting room the grown-ups huddle over the hole, trying to get a glimpse of what is down there.

'Can you see anything?' asks Jimmy impatiently. It's too early to answer back.

When he shines the light of the torch around they get an idea of the space they're in. It is like a normal room in a house, except that there is no daylight and all shapes are draped in velvet blackness. The torchlight moves over a dresser against a wall with a jug and old plates, covered in dust. It lights up a small desk with a single chair behind it and next to it a mirror on the wall, covered in spider threads. The torch reveals a door of a cupboard built into the wall. In the far corner of the room the light beam finds what looks like a granite plinth. On top of it is a kind of cup or bowl. It has the shape of a large egg, but much bigger and cut in half. There's something about it that draws his attention. He steps closer to it. The torch lights up the number seven carved in the plinth. Then he realises that this is the seventh stone, this plinth. This one is the real seventh stone, not the slate in the sitting room above in which his father had carved his name. So is this his fortune? This peculiar stone cup? Is this his inheritance?

'Steven, look!' says Isabella. 'There's a letter on the desk.' He shines the light back to the desk to where Isabella points. He sees the letter. It's sealed like the document he was given in Mr Liddell's office. In Thomas Carpenter's unmistakable handwriting it reads: 'To My Rightful Heir'.

'What have you found?' comes Jimmy's impatient call again from above.

'Wait,' Isabella calls back. 'There is a whole room down here. We're still looking. We've found a letter.'

He feels small and important at the same time. He is calm and serious. He takes the sealed letter, blows off the dust and breaks the seal.

'Can you shine the torch?' he asks. He hands the torch to Joey. With Joey and Isabella standing behind him and looking over his shoulder he unfolds the paper. It is one sheet of paper, filled with the familiar marks of Thomas Carpenter's pen. By the light of the torch they read it together.

September 24th, of the Year 1892
To My Rightful Heir

I regret I do not have the privilege of knowing you, my rightful heir, nor do I know your name or the time when you will be standing here to claim the fortune that I transfer by the law and my Last Will to you. I hope and pray that you, who have come here, are indeed my rightful heir. If you have followed the path of my seven stones, I know you will be worthy.

I remind you, as stated in my testament, that if you expect to find silver or gold you are to be disappointed. The fortune I give you - of far greater value as you will discover when the time is right - is the stone cup you see in this room. Close your hands around it, keep it safe. See beyond the surface, believe in what you see!

I ask forgiveness for my eccentricity and for the magic of words that I have applied to guard this fortune. You are here now. You have stood the test. I will rest peacefully with my beloved Clara and be at one with the mystery of this world. Everything must have its course, a journey for each one of us is written in the stars. My journey is ending. Yours may just begin.

I also leave you this casket on the desk. You have the key. The casket contains a precious book, a diary by the King, who visited the Estate on the river when I was a younger man. How this book came into my possession is too much to explain here. I ask that you treat it with dignity. This manuscript is important! Its significance will become evident in time.

So this is my last note to you, my heir. Stories end and stories begin. Many lives may be lived between you and me. So much mystery remains hidden. The truth lives in a pure heart. Only some are meant to see.

In gratitude,
Thomas Carpenter

He looks at his friends. The letter is as mysterious as Thomas Carpenter's earlier riddles hidden in the seven stones. Has he found the fortune? According to what they just read he has. He feels the significance of the situation, the solemn meaning of Thomas Carpenter's last note. But what that meaning is, he doesn't understand.

He walks over to the object on the granite plinth in the corner of the room. He closes both his hands around the cup and lifts it. It is heavier than it looks.

'Will you take the casket?' he asks Isabella. She nodds.

He makes his way back to the ladder, the cup clasped to

his chest. 'We are coming back up,' he calls out.

In Thomas Carpenter's day Wheal Argon was a working mine, just like Drakewalls. Greystone House must have been a hive of activity, a constant coming and going. In the days following Steven's discovery of the seventh stone it gets busy again. Historical and archaeological experts visit their house to examine the underground room that has been untouched and unchanged for a hundred and twentytwo years. The door that he had noticed turns out not to be a cupboard, but a door giving access to an underground tunnel straight into the heart of the old Wheal Argon mine. From his house, the mine captain Thomas Carpenter was directly connected with the network of excavations. Mining experts now come to carry out inspections. To his mum's relief the construction of the tunnel is declared completely safe and stable. If not, it would have left Greystone House practically worthless and impossible to sell. He almost hoped that would have happened, but of course they would have ended up with even bigger money problems.

There is also much interest from the press, not just from the local press, but from national newspapers and television stations too. 'Secrets of Mining History Unearthed' reads one headline. Another newspaper reveals: 'Thirteen Year Old Digs Deep for Royal History.' He and his mum have to do one interview after the other. Luckily his stutter stays away. They have cancelled the new appointment with the surgeon.

He asks the others not to mention anything about the inheritance, should any of the reporters want to know, and not to say anything publicly about the stone cup. He doesn't know why. He just feels it's important not to talk about it, at least until he understands better what Thomas Carpenter meant about the cup and its value. So if any of the journalists want to know how they discovered the hidden room they say that it happened by accident, or that his cat had found it. 'Kasparov Makes Winning Move' claims the Thornbridge Gazette.

'You have the key' Thomas Carpenter had written and Steven knew what he meant. Upstairs in his room was the key he retrieved from Thomas Carpenter's gravestone, the key that opened the wooden box with his testament in Mr Liddell's office. On the evening of the party he fetched it straight away. As he expected the key also fitted the lock of the wooden casket. Inside was a thick volume with handwritten diary notes of King Henry-George. Sandy was in no doubt that they were real. She recognized the King's signature. He knew immediately what he should do and told Sandy he wanted Oakendale Castle to have the document. It was the least he could do to make some good for the damage caused by the fire. The National Trust would be able to look after the manuscript professionally. Sandy had been delighted. She knew the King's diary would be a huge attraction for future visitors to the restored house and tower.

On 30th December peace at Greystone House has finally returned. Experts and journalists have exhausted their investigations and reporting. At last Steven and his mum have the house to themselves again. His mum couldn't be in a better mood. This morning a letter from

Jimmy arrived in the post. He saw it had a cheque inside. He didn't see the amount, but from his mum's gasp he could tell it was a lot. Enough not to have to sell Greystone House!

His mum has promised to make pizzas again. He would have liked to go over to Isabella, but she has already gone up to London with her mum and dad for the Blue River Dreams performance tomorrow night.

Steven sits at the table with Kasparov on his lap and his chess pieces on the board in front of him. He doesn't make a move. His mind travels back through the events of the last three months. His quest is completed. With some determination and a lot of luck he has solved the challenging puzzle that Thomas Carpenter had laid out for him. He has found the seven stones. They have found them. It was a proper test, like in the stories of King Arthur. But many questions remain. Why has all this happened to him? Why did he, by accident, become the heir to someone living so long ago, of whose existence he had no idea? The old solicitor in his letter to Steven wrote about things that are meant to be and destiny finding you. That might be true, but it offers no explanation. There have been so many strange coincidences. Looking for the road to Penny Cross for example, at exactly the right time of year to find the second stone on the fifth of November. And what about the broken man? How could Thomas Carpenter have foreseen Jimmy in a wheelchair, or Miss Henderson on horseback above at Eden Farm? How could Thomas Carpenter have predicted the fire at Oakendale Castle and, strangest of all, how did his name turn out to be an anagram of the seventh stone? The fortune he had been looking for was here all the time, right under his nose in Greystone House. He wonders about the message lost in the fire. Would it have said anything about Kasparov finding the fortune?

He also thinks about the old solicitor, Mr Liddell. Is he the man in his dreams. Where has he gone? He would so much like to meet the old man again, to tell him about everything that happened since he and Isabella had come to the office in Thornbridge. Would Mr Liddell know anything more about the stone cup?

17 Midnight Express

It's 31st December 2014. The musicians of Blue River Dreams are waiting in the wings at the New Black Bean Festival, the national festival showcasing new musical talent. Their instruments are already on stage, except for Joey's drumsticks, which he is flicking nervously in his hands. Isabella catches a glimpse of the audience through the curtains. Her eyes find her mum and dad in the third row and next to them Steven and his mum. Everybody is chatting. Nobody in the audience can see her here behind the curtains, waiting nervously.

One hundred and twentytwo years, three months and some days earlier, an old man sits behind a desk in a room, lit by the glow of an oil lamp and a candle. It is close to midnight. The man has silver white hair and large hands. From his hands you can tell that he has been strong, even though they are now wrinkled and marked by age. He writes his name under the letter he has written, puts down his pen and blows on the ink to dry it. Then he folds the paper, takes the pen again and writes 'To My Rightful Heir' on the outside. After that he drips candle wax on to it where the edges of the paper meet, waits for the wax to harden and places the letter in the middle of the desk.

He stands up, blows out the candle, takes the oil lamp and walks to a corner of the room where a stone cup is placed on a plinth. He hangs the oil lamp on a hook, takes a jug from the dresser and pours water into the stone cup. He puts the jug back. He closes his hands around the cup, lifts it nearer to his face and waits until the surface of the water becomes still. He looks.

He sees a boy. The boy runs into the cemetery. Two other boys chase him. They lose sight of him. He runs to the gate. The gate is closed. The other two hold him down. They push him and he falls backwards, his head against the gravestone. Is he alive? The other two disappear. The church bells ring but there is no sound.

The man sighs. He places the cup back carefully. He takes the oil lamp and walks to the ladder on the other side of the room. He looks back one more time. His eyes say goodbye to the object on the granite plinth, before he resolutely steps on to the ladder and climbs up, holding the oil lamp in one hand. In the room above he closes the panel in the floor. The hearthstone of slate lies ready. With the expertise of a man who knows how to move stones and with considerable effort given his age, he pushes the slate over the floor until it sinks perfectly in its place over the panel, as if it has always been there.

Last week he checked progress with the stone carver working on his headstone. He is content that the work has been done exactly as he instructed. The arrangements with his solicitors Clarke and Liddell have been in place since June. All is now prepared.

He takes the oil lamp again and walks the steps up to his bedroom. He places the oil lamp on the stool beside his bed and lays himself to rest. With his hand he turns down the wick in the lamp to extinguish the flame. He lets the night sleep come over him.

James Black moves his wheelchair centre stage and takes

the microphone. They know who he is. He waits until the applause ceases before he speaks.

'Ladies and Gentlemen, it is with enormous pride and pleasure that I present to you one of the youngest bands ever to perform here. One of the youngest and one of the most exciting! Put your hands together please for Blue River Dreams.'

The spotlights flick on. The five walk on stage. Isabella takes the microphone, closes her eyes and waits for the music to begin.

ACKNOWLEDGEMENTS

I'm enormously grateful to Maudie Smith, Catherine Sandbrook, Nic Vos de Wael, Zr. Dionne Appelman, my mother Rie Ursem-Appelman, Li Selman, Dorigen Couchman, Marianne Bos-Clark and Archie Clark, who helped me through their encouraging comments and critical reading, and to Sally McLaren and David Webster, in whose homely cottage I started writing 'the Seventh Stone'.

Big thanks most of all to my most wonderful wife Helen Porter, for seeing me and always believing in me.

ABOUT PETRUS URSEM

Petrus Ursem was born in The Netherlands, the youngest son in a family of nine children. From his father he learned to play with words and turn them inside out. His mother taught him to listen and observe. On joining the newsletter team at his secondary school he discovered his pleasure in writing.

Petrus studied literature at the University of Utrecht, then worked as a writer in the world of education whilst studying fine art in The Hague. When he moved to England his creative work as a painter and printmaker took flight.

His move to Cornwall in 2011 rekindled his desire to write children's novels. He lives in the Tamar Valley, not far from Steven.

www.peterursem.co.uk

Steven's adventures and
the Thomas Carpenter Affair will continue
in "The Truth Teller"